ALEX

SISTERS BY DESIGN

SHARON SROCK

For my granddaughter, Abigail, the independent, surefooted one. You have dreams for the future. Hold them tight and never let anyone convince you that you can't do what you've set your mind to.

But let all those that put their trust in thee rejoice: let them ever shout for joy, because thou defendest them: let them also that love thy name be joyful in thee.

For thou, Lord, will bless the righteous; with favour wilt thou compass him as with a shield.

Psalms 5: 11-12

ACKNOWLEDGMENTS

Father, thank You for once again filling my head with characters and ideas. I hope I turned it into a story that glorifies You and expresses Your love for us.

Many thanks to Shel Harrington, family law attorney and fellow OCFW member. She walked me through the maze of Oklahoma's divorce laws and helped me find the perfect answer when I thought I'd written myself into a corner. Any mistakes you find in that area are totally mine.

I have so many great people who contribute to the production of my stories. Critique partner, Terri Weldon, editor, Robin Patchen, proofreaders, Judy DeVries and Elizabeth Lopez, cover designer, Samantha Fury, prayer partners too numerous to list, and a whole group of pre-readers who make sure there are reviews on release day. I couldn't do this without you. There aren't enough ways to say thanks, but I hope each of you knows how valuable you are, how much your support and input means to me.

ONE

Divorced?

Alexandra Conklin looked at the papers her son had just spread out on the dining room table. She jerked her hands into her lap and twisted the thin silver band on her left hand. As long as she didn't touch them, maybe they wouldn't be real. Hard to deny the presence of her signature, though, and Hunter's. It made no sense. They'd fixed that more than two decades ago.

Hadn't they?

She looked up at her husband. Hunter sat across the table, his expression no less confused than hers.

"Mom, Dad?" Older by four minutes, Benjamin took the lead while his twin, Sean, sat back, arms crossed against his chest, his eyes moving from one parent to another.

Hunter crossed his own arms and sent Alex a hooded glance before speaking. "Where did you get this?"

The boys looked at each other. Something passed between them...some twin communication Alex had never been able to understand or participate in. A look, a twitch, a shrug. Benjamin spoke again.

"Your anniversary is coming up in a couple of weeks."

"Three," Alex said.

"Whatever." Benjamin's single word was filled with frustration. "We wanted to surprise you with a special gift. We needed a copy of your marriage license. Since we didn't want you suspicious, we went to the courthouse to get it. The clerk asked us if we wanted a copy of the divorce filing as well."

Another look at Sean, and the younger boy spoke for the first time. "How could we say no?"

Alex sat back and looked at Hunter. "Did you know about this?"

"Don't be ridiculous," he snapped.

Well, they didn't agree on much these days, but at least they were on the same page here. A rather dumfounded page.

Benjamin leaned on the edge of the table and tapped the papers. "Are you telling us that you didn't know about this?"

Sean mirrored his brother's pose. "Those certainly look like your signatures."

"Yep, I got pretty good at forging your name when we were in junior high." Benjamin sent his mother a sarcastic smile. "But if this is a forgery, it's a professional job."

Alex stared at her sons, distracted by the forgery statement for a second. She gave her head a tiny shake and brought herself back on track. Her sons were adults now, beyond grounding for an adolescent prank, and concerned about something much more serious. Tonight had been their once-a-month Tuesday dinner. Something Alex looked forward to every month. Not just because the twins made it a point to save the night for family time, but because she could count on Hunter to be home at a decent time. Her sons, both finishing up their sophomore year at the University of Oklahoma, had seemed distant and preoccupied ever since they'd arrived. Had this moment of confrontation been on their minds all through dinner? She looked at Hunter, expecting him to take the lead. Her expectations died when he expelled a heavy breath, lowered his head into his hands, and rubbed his temples.

The reaction didn't surprise her. Hunter could handle the five hundred members of his congregation with the ease of a conductor directing a symphony, but parenting had always been just a half step beyond his reach. Not that he didn't love his boys—he did. But for most of their life he'd been the occasional cheerleader, the wait-until-your-father-gets-home disciplinarian, or the absentminded granter of favors instead of the day-to-day, down-in-the-trenches parent. That job belonged to Alex.

"Mom," the boys said in unison. They understood where their answers would come from.

"Yes, your father and I signed those papers. We also called the lawyer and told him that we'd changed our minds."

"I don't think he got the message," Benjamin quipped.

"This isn't funny," Sean barked at his brother in a rare display of annoyance.

"Throttle down, bro, I'm not laughing," Benjamin said. "Just stating the obvious."

"Boys." Alex gathered the papers and tapped them together. "Not now."

"Wait." Benjamin motioned to them. "What are you doing?"

"Your father and I will get to the bottom of this once the county offices open in the morning."

"And you think Sean and I are just going to go back to school tonight and pretend this didn't happen?"

The thought...hope...had crossed her mind. Instead, the boys exchanged a frown, settled into their chairs like their butts had been sown to the cushions, and fixed identical stares on Alex. The confusion in their expressions twisted Alex's heart. Maybe if she downplayed it...

"There's nothing to tell. This is obviously a clerical error of some sort. I'll get to the bottom of it. I'll let you guys know—"

"Nothing to tell?" Benjamin's expression was an exact replica of the don't-mess-with-me face Alex had used on them their entire life. "We don't even know if our parents are married or not. How is that not important?"

"What he said." Sean wagged a finger between his parents. "You guys got married, changed your minds, filed for divorce, and changed your minds again? An explanation seems appropriate, 'cause I sure don't remember you ever being that indecisive when it came to making decisions for us."

After another unproductive look at Hunter, Alex surrendered with a sigh and gave them the abbreviated version of the story. "Your father and I married very young. I was barely twenty-three and he was twenty-four. I was teaching first grade in the city, and your father had just moved to town to take the youth pastor position at the church I was attending."

Alex glanced at Hunter from under her eyelashes. She longed to feel the zing of attraction that'd charged the very air around them all those years ago. She waited in vain. Somewhere, the fire between them had been tamped down to polite distance. This wasn't a new revelation for Alex, but it still stung. It'd been love-at-first-sight for them, followed by a whirlwind courtship and an elopement four months later. Hunter Conklin had been everything she'd ever dreamed of. A smart, good looking Christian boy who wanted to change the world for God. So did she. It was their individual approach to that task that got them into trouble.

"You guys were youth pastors for five years," Sean said, "and then Dad got the opportunity for the assistant pastor position here in Garfield."

"He moved up to senior pastor three years later," Benjamin added. "We know all that. We lived it."

"We married in the spring," Alex said, "four months after we met. Just me and your father, alone in the judge's chambers with the judge and his secretary for a witness. No music, no flowers, nothing fancy. I don't have a single picture of the ceremony. When school started again in the fall, Dad wanted me to stay home, and I wanted to return to my teaching position. We hadn't discussed my job. I suppose we...I... just thought life would go on as a couple like it had as singles." She clutched the papers in her lap. "It wasn't quite that simple."

Her hand trembled when she lifted her glass to sip at her tea. "He wanted me to give up the career I'd trained for, one I loved, to be a full-time minister's wife. I didn't see the need. I love the ministry and certainly wanted to be as much help to your father as possible, but he wasn't making a lot of money, and there was so little I could do at the church." She shrugged. "I wanted to teach for a couple more years. I thought my calling, at least part of it, was ministering to the kids in my class. We fought about it. We couldn't resolve it. We decided to go our separate ways. Once we realized divorce wasn't a part of God's plan, we called it off. End of story."

Silence fell around the table.

"The whys aren't important," Alex assured them. "All that matters is that, once we realized our mistake, we fixed it." She waved the bundle of folded papers. "Or so we thought."

"So you're not worried about not being married?" Sean asked.

"It's not an issue." Finally, Hunter spoke up. "We've always been married in the eyes of God. A piece of paper doesn't change that, especially a piece of paper we didn't know existed." When Benjamin opened his mouth, Hunter held up a hand to silence him. "I understand that there are valid legal reasons for marriages being documented by the state. I agree with them, but it doesn't change the facts. Your mother and I have been married for almost twenty-three years regardless of what a misfiled piece of paper has to say about it."

Benjamin held his hand across the table. "Can I have those back for a minute?" Once Alex passed them over, he spread them out on the table a second time and studied them. He looked at his mom and dad and then at his brother. "God changed your mind about the divorce?"

Alex nodded over the churning in her stomach.

"These papers are dated six months before Sean and I were born. Did God change your mind, or did being pregnant change your mind?"

Alex closed her eyes. Her precious baby boys had grown into intelligent young men. She had no one but herself to blame if they'd outsmarted her. "I'd call finding out you were having twins God's final word on the subject, wouldn't you?"

ALEX CRAWLED into bed five minutes behind Hunter. His back was to her, and she couldn't see if his eyes were open or closed, she didn't care. They needed to talk whether he wanted to or not. She nudged his shoulder.

"Hunter, you can't possibly be asleep. I know we tried to minimize this situation for the boys, but we need to talk."

He rolled to his back, eyes still closed, hands clasped at his waist. "I'm tired. I worked like a madman in order to finish up and be home for your dinner tonight. There's nothing about this that can't wait until morning."

Alex remained braced on an arm while she studied her husband in the dim light of the bedside lamp. His hairline had receded in the last few years, but not much gray had threaded through the brown yet. His handsome face boasted a chiseled nose, finely drawn lips, and his jawline had an attractive end-of-day scruff. Behind his closed lids lurked dark green eyes the exact shade of a weathered emerald. Members of their congregation often commented that Hunter's eyes could bore straight through to your soul. God had blessed him with a gift of deep discernment. A pity his gift faded to dormant when it came to his family.

"I want to talk about it tonight," she said. "This is serious. I thought you contacted the lawyer and halted the divorce proceedings."

Hunter tossed the sheet aside, slid up against the headboard, and crossed his arms over his bare chest. "So this is my fault?"

Alex stared at the man she'd been married to...thought she'd been married to, for half her life. "I think assigning fault is less important than discussing a solution."

Hunter finally turned to face her. His green eyes remained calm. His whole aspect was one of unconcern. "I called the lawyer the day you told me you were pregnant.

We were well within the six months that Oklahoma gives you. He said he'd take care of it. I had no reason to doubt his word. He probably did. You said yourself this must be a clerical error of some sort."

"What if it's not?" How could he be so unconcerned?

"Then we'll fix it."

"You mean we'll get remarried."

"If that's what it takes." He narrowed his eyes. "In the meantime, I expect you to keep this business to yourself. I meant what I told the boys. Our marriage vows were a covenant before God. A piece of paper doesn't break that. Nevertheless, there are some in the church who might be offended to find out that the pastor they respect once considered divorce, even worse carried through with it. I've worked too hard for too long to have what I've built threatened by senseless gossip."

The *pastor* they respect? *He'd* worked? Indignation crawled up Alex's spine and drew the corners of her mouth tight. Of all the self-serving...condescending..."*We.* You mean we've worked, right?"

"Yes, Alex, we." He brushed her concerns aside with a sweep of his hand. "This is a delicate issue. I hope I don't need to remind you that your silence needs to include that group of women you run with."

"The women I..." Alex sputtered to a stop. Sometimes his attitude made her angry enough to pull out her own hair. She chose to carve some time out of her week for a social life. He didn't. Each was a personal choice. Neither was wrong, except that his choice to be busy twenty hours out of twenty-four left his wife feeling neglected and alone. He wouldn't think of that though, not with a *higher calling* on his time. "Those women you're referring to are all God-fearing, faithful members of *our* congregation. Yes, we share among ourselves, but you couldn't torture a confidence out of any of them if you tried. You needn't worry, though. I'm aware of my place as a pastor's wife."

Silence settled between them for a few seconds. Eighteen inches of mattress separated them. It felt more like a yawning chasm. Hunter reached across the small space and took her hand. In a rare show of physical affection, he lifted it to his lips and brushed a kiss across her knuckles, his voice conciliatory when he said, "I didn't mean to sound harsh or dismissive. You've been a wonderful pastor's wife." He let go of her hand and smoothed the sheet where it lay across his waist. "I know most of your concern is for the boys. They're upset, and I'm sorry for that, but once we put this behind us, they'll be OK."

"I think the timing hurt them." Alex settled on to her pillow. "Thinking that we got back together just for them."

"Is that a bad thing? They're not little boys anymore. Maybe it's time for you to let them be men."

Irritation pricked a second time. Hunter, the barely-there father, Hunter who couldn't tell her either boy's favorite sport or favorite meal or how they liked their eggs, was going to tell her to let the sons she'd raised be men. "How could you sit across the table from them and be so clueless?"

"What are you talking about?"

How could he have missed the hurt and confusion on their faces? Like lost little boys. *How could he?* Because Hunter Conklin had ceased to consider earthly things years before. The reminder saddened her. The reminder infuriated her. Not bothering to respond, Alex twisted out of the bed and grabbed her pillow.

"What are you doing?"

"I'm going to the guest room. I'm not sleeping with a

clueless, maybe husband." She slammed the door on her way out.

———

ACROSS TOWN in the darkened bedroom of Lisa and Dave Sisko, the Pastors of Valley View Church, Lisa raised her head from her husband's chest. "Dave?"

"I'm awake. I have been for a few minutes."

"Is God nudging you to pray too?"

His arm tightened around her. "Yep."

"Alex and Hunter?"

"Yep."

Lisa settled her head back against the pillow of Dave's chest. "Jesus…" she whispered.

Dave's voice was a soft rumble in her ear. "Father, we don't know the situation, but You do. You were concerned enough to wake us up and call us to prayer. Please bring peace and comfort to our friends."

TWO

Alex turned over in the bed, moving with innate care so as not to wake Hunter. She stretched and cracked one eye open. The mid-April dawn shed just enough light through the window to cast the details of the room in shadow. She froze. What was she doing in the guest room? She stretched her hand across the mattress and met the smooth, cool sheets of an unused space. *What...?* The memory of yesterday's talk with the boys and Hunter's unfailingly clueless attitude slammed into her with the force of flood waters against a dam.

Oh, yeah. They were divorced...maybe. Alex fumbled on the nightstand for her phone and pressed the button to illuminate the screen and time display. Almost six-thirty. She threw the covers aside. She needed to get Hunter up and start his breakfast. Her husband likely had a full calendar for the day—he always did—but if they were at the courthouse when the doors unlocked at eight, maybe they could get to the bottom of this mess quickly and get him on his way. If this morning's business took too long, there was no telling how late his day would run. She'd need to reschedule her morning as well, let Mac know she'd miss their workout session.

That brought a chuckle. Her thirty-nine-year-old friend was due to deliver twins in the next six weeks. Alex, having carried twins herself, didn't expect Mac to make it to her due date. But so far, Mac had been very blessed. She hadn't been confined to bed as Alex had for the last eight weeks of her pregnancy. Regardless, she spent less and less time at the spa these days. She'd suspended all exercise classes at Soeur's right after the new year, claiming *the belly* couldn't take the steep climb to the second floor workout area multiple times in a day. Mac managed to put in a brief daily appearance on the ground floor of her business and only braved the stairs three times a week when her friends gathered for their workout sessions. She sat and barked orders while the others took turns leading the workout. Alex shuddered. She understood Mac's desire to spend some time with her friends, but Alex had frequent nightmares about Mac's water breaking at the top of those steep, narrow stairs, and the five of them not being able to get her down quickly enough. Those exercise mats would make a very uncomfortable birthing bed if the babies chose to make their escape at the wrong time.

Alex set her worries about Mac aside and stepped into the master bedroom. The bed was unmade but empty. She peeked into the adjoining bathroom, which was also empty, but two wet towels littered the floor. *Good grief.* She stooped to pick them up, folded them, and draped them over the bar of the rack to dry. How much trouble was that, really? She blew out a breath. Almost twenty-three years together, and her husband still had the household manners of a six-year-old.

But...if her husband was up and about so early, maybe

he was more disturbed by the boys' revelation last night than he'd let on. As sad as Alex was to admit it, the idea of Hunter having a restless night lifted some of the weight off her own shoulders. It meant he was just as troubled as she was. She drew the comforter up to the head of the bed, fluffed the pillows, and arranged them to her liking. Bed making, another chore Hunter never got the hang of. The sound of the garage door closing drew her to the window just in time to see his car pull away from the curb.

But...

Alex hurried to the kitchen. Where was he going so early? They had important things to take care of. He couldn't possibly have forgotten, could he? A piece of notepaper sat propped against his empty coffee cup. She plucked it up and carried it to the stove so she could read it in the light of the vent hood.

I had a call from Ed Robbins this morning. His mother had a bad night, and he asked me to come pray with them. Let me know what you find out at the courthouse.

She crumpled the note in her hand. Of all the... Hazel Robbins was ninety years old and as healthy as a horse despite her dementia. A bad night for her didn't involve any physical ailment. A bad night for Hazel meant sitting up in her recliner all night, flipping through old picture albums, singing tearful lullabies to old baby pictures. Once the staff of the nursing home brought her breakfast, she'd eat and sleep the day away. Hazel had a *bad night* a dozen times a month. Alex stared out the window and watched the world lighten with the rising sun. As bad as she might feel for Hazel and her family, Hazel's bad night didn't qualify as an emergency for Hunter. It was an excuse. Conscience pricked her pastor's wife heart, and Alex closed her eyes.

Sorry, Father. You know I love Hazel like my own

mother. I lift her up to You again this morning. Grant her peace. Comfort her family. Have Your will in all their lives. The crumpled paper bit into Alex's hand, and she realized she was still squeezing it for all she was worth. She relaxed her grip and hoped Hazel had a good day. A better day than Alex was going to have as she tried to figure out the status of her marriage, alone. *Father, I need Your will in our lives today too. Please calm my frustrations and help me find the answers we...I...need.*

HUNTER JOINED ED in the corridor of the nursing home.

Ed held out his hand. "Thanks for coming, Pastor."

Hunter took the proffered hand in a firm grasp. "Absolutely. How is she?"

Ed's eyes cut to the closed door of his mother's room. Concerned lined his sixty-year-old face. "She's still crying and singing and rocking. The nurses tried to get her back to bed, but she's ignoring them. I tried, too, but she just looked at me as if she didn't know who I was. I'm sorry to bother you so early on a Wednesday morning, I just..."

"This is a difficult time for your family. I don't know what I can do to help, but let's go in and take a stab at it."

Ed pushed the door open a few inches. "Mom, you have a visitor."

The old woman in the chair didn't even look up. Her voice, raspy with age and heavy with tears, filled the room with the off-key words of an old lullaby.

"Lavender blue and rosemary green,
When I am king you shall be queen;
Call up my maids at four o'clock,

Some to the wheel and some to the rock;
Some to make hay and some to shear corn,
And you and I will keep the bed warm."

Ed motioned for Hunter to follow him into the room. He stood beside the chair as the singing continued. "It's as if she doesn't even know we're here."

Hunter crossed the small space and crouched down next to the chair. He took a few seconds to study the pictures the old woman caressed as she sang. Pictures of a dark-haired little girl wearing a fancy dress and shiny white shoes. Next to her stood a boy, a couple of years younger, dressed in black pants and a white shirt, a bowtie just under his chin. Both held Easter baskets and beamed for the camera. He looked up at Ed.

"Me and my sister, Kathy." He tilted his head. "More than fifty years ago."

Hunter placed a hand over the old woman's gnarled knuckles. When he spoke, his voice was pitched low and soothing. "My goodness, Hazel. Those are lovely children."

The old woman's singing stopped mid-verse as she peered up at Hunter with cloudy eyes. "They're good babies. Have you seen them?"

Hunter ignored Ed's whispered, "Mom."

"They do look familiar. May I take a closer look?"

Hazel pushed the album closer to Hunter. He took it, held it to the light, and flipped a few pages. "You know, I think I saw this young man out in the hall helping the nurses deliver breakfast trays."

Hazel nodded. "Probably so, he's a good, helpful boy."

Hunter put the book aside and held out his hand. "Let me help you back to your bed. I can smell your breakfast. Why don't you get started on your tray, and I'll go see if I can find him for you?"

Hazel took his hand, and Hunter helped her stand. Ed hurried to take her other arm. She looked around at the touch, and her face split into a smile. "Well, here's my Eddie. You don't have to go lookin' for him." Hazel leaned into her son, her head coming just to his shoulder. She lifted her face. "You have a kiss for your mamma?"

"Yes, ma'am." Ed bent and kissed the top of her head. "Are you hungry?"

"Well, yes. They brought my breakfast some time ago, but I was waiting on you. What took you so long?"

Ed looked over Hazel's head and mouthed a *thank you.*

Hunter shook his head and helped Hazel settle in with her meal.

She picked up her fork and hesitated. "Pastor, I'd be pleased if you blessed my meal."

Hunter rubbed his forehead. It looked as if Hazel's mind had come back to the present. "I'd be happy to." He placed a hand on the old woman's shoulder. "Father God, we give You thanks for this glorious day and this fine meal You've provided for Sister Hazel. Lord, we ask that You'd be with her today. Give her continued health and clarity. Give her family peace and wisdom. We ask these things in the name of your son, Jesus."

"Amen." Hazel forked up a bite of scrambled eggs. She touched them to her tongue, frowned, and put them down. "Ed, get my salt and pepper out of my drawer. You know I can't eat this bland stuff."

"Yes, ma'am," Ed went to do as she asked. He put the condiments on the tray and followed Hunter out the door. "Thanks again, Pastor. I never know what it's going to take to pull her back to reality."

"I'm not sure what I did, but if you think it helped, that's all the thanks I need. Now go back in and enjoy your mother before she slips away again." Hunter exited the nursing home and looked at his watch. Seven-thirty. He'd swing by the Sonic and grab a coffee and a breakfast sandwich before settling into his office for the morning. Once the administrative stuff was out of the way, he had hospital visits to make. Grace Community was growing, and, with the membership tipping towards five hundred, there were always a few in the hospital. Today, he had four members split between three hospitals in a fifty-mile radius. If he hurried, he could be finished by two. Then he'd have a couple of hours to finalize his Wednesday night sermon before his two counseling sessions. And somewhere in there he had to finish the missions report for the district and look over next quarter's Sunday school curriculum. A full day, but nothing filled his spirit with more joy than doing what God had called him to do. *Thank you, Father, for allowing me one more day to work for You.*

HUNTER'S unexpected departure gave Alex the perfect excuse to stick to her normal Wednesday schedule. The workout would clear her head and get her blood pumping. And even though she couldn't, as Hunter had been so quick to warn her, share the details of the situation, a few minutes with her friends would get some prayer flowing in the right direction.

Alex mulled that while she tied her shoes. Maybe she was blowing things out of proportion. There wasn't really any *situation* to pray about yet, and there might not ever be. This just had to be some sort of clerical error like they'd told the boys. She closed her eyes, her hand resting on the front doorknob. *Please, let it be a simple mistake.*

Twenty minutes later, Alex parked in front of the spa. She grinned at the sight of Dane's truck occupying the space next to hers. With D-day so close, Mac's husband was sticking to her side like glue. His concentrated attention was driving Mac a little crazy, but Alex thought it was sweet. Seeing them together always brought back fond memories of her own pregnancy. Days when Hunter hovered over her with the same loving concern.

She entered the spa and stopped short when she saw Mackenzie Cooper, the spa's very pregnant business owner, leaning against the wall next to the stairs, head down, eyes closed, her hands clasped under the girth of a belly that had grown bigger since Alex'd seen it two days before.

Alarm drove Alex across the room at a run. "Mac, what is it?"

Mac's weary blue eyes snapped open. "Hey." She glanced at the door. "I didn't hear the bell."

"Are you OK?"

"What...? Oh." She grinned and rested a hand on the mound of her belly. "Just giving the storkletts a little pre-climb pep talk. They're pretty busy in there. I was reminding them that it's just fifteen steps. If they're good for the next hour or so, they get a milkshake after you guys leave."

Alex put a hand next to Mac's, smiling when the babies shifted beneath her touch. "*They* get a milkshake?"

"Oh, yeah, they're all about vicarious pleasures these days. They love it when I listen to music, they jump up and down for joy when it's time for me to take a nap, and when their daddy rubs my feet at the end of a long day, I can almost hear them purr."

"Speaking of 'daddy,' where is he? His van is outside."

"Next door," Mac answered. "Did I tell you guys that we bought the retail space next to the spa?"

"You did."

"That's good. There are days lately when I can't remember my own name. Anyway, there's a person interested in renting it for a craft store. Umm." Mac frowned. "Crafted with Love, Dane called it. Not craft supplies, but more of a gift shop. The newest addition to Garfield's downtown revival. She plans to feature items from local crafters."

"That's a lovely idea," Alex said.

"Yeah, and we won't talk about the fact that, while Dane is working next door, he's out from under my feet."

"He's just watching out for his family." Alex nodded toward the stairs. "You ready?"

Mac glanced up the steep stairs and pulled in a bracing breath.

"You don't have to go up there."

"Yes, I do. I'm on a two hundred seventy step countdown."

Alex tilted her head.

"Fifteen steps, three times a week, for the next six weeks. That totals two hundred seventy until D-day," Mac straightened. "And then there's the milkshake."

Alex laughed, leaned closer, and spoke to the belly. "Chocolate milkshake." She pulled back when her hand received a solid thump.

"Told you."

"Hmm..." Alex offered Mac an arm. "Let's go, Mommy, slow and steady. Are the others waiting?"

"Yes," Mac answered. "I needed the bathroom before I climbed Everest." With one hand on the rail and the other clasped around Alex's arm, they cleared the halfway point and stopped for a breath. Mac leaned into Alex. "Can I tell you a secret before we get in there with the cop?"

"Sure."

"If my doctor lets me go one day past my due date, he's a dead man."

Alex took a firmer grip on her friend's arm as they continued up the steps. "Justifiable homicide, girl. Charley would probably loan you her gun."

Alex opened the door at the top of the steps and stayed close to Mac while she lowered herself into a chair.

"She OK?" The *cop*, Charlene Hubbard, shelved a set of hand weights and pushed sweat dampened strands of her short, blond hair out of her face.

"She's fine," Alex answered. "Just a little out of breath."

Miranda Page tightened the band holding her thick red hair back from her face while her cool green eyes studied Mac. "Girlfriend, you don't have any business making that climb. We can do this without you until those babies get here."

Sydney Patterson handed the mom-to-be a bottle of cold water from the mini-fridge in the corner. "What she said. There's no need to wear yourself out so early in the day."

"Syd, Randy, leave the woman alone, will you? That's my niece and nephew in there, and if climbing those stairs gets them here a little faster, we'll exercise five days a week." Jessica Saxton pushed her ever-sagging glasses back into place, crouched down next to Mac, and placed both hands on Mac's swollen belly. "Good morning, Forrest and Brook. I can't wait to meet you."

Mac cringed. "Don't call them that."

Jesse sat back on her heels. "But you just said yesterday—"

"I know, but I think we're going with Aria and Adam now."

Jesse cocked her head. "Really? It was Sarah and Samuel last week, Grace and Tucker on Sunday, Forrest and Brook yesterday. You guys have to make up your minds."

"We've still got six weeks." Mac's tone was defensive. "It's hard to name one baby, much less two." Her gaze went from Alex to Syd to Charley in turn. "You guys went through this. Tell her."

"Sarah and Samuel are still my favorites," Randy said, "but you discarded those days ago."

Jesse waved the redhead's opinion away. "We don't care what you think. Your kid came with a name."

Randy laughed. "I guess you're right about that. But I can't imagine Astor being anything but an Astor."

"That's exactly what we want," Mac said. "Whatever we decide on, we need to be able to look at them ten years from now and say that's who they are. It's a big responsibility."

"Speaking of responsibility." Charley took Mac's normal position at the front of the room. "I'm your leader for today, so let's get this show on the road. I have patrol in an hour."

Alex joined her friends in the center of the mat-covered floor as Charley led them in some opening stretches. Being with these women was the best medicine in the world. They made her feel good. She bent to touch her toes, then strained the extra distance to lay her hands flat on the floor. She was forty-six years old, and she could still touch the floor without bending her knees. Suddenly her trip to the courthouse didn't seem so daunting.

THREE

Alex looked at the paperwork laid out on Harrison Lake's desk, her heart thumping at the opinion the lawyer had just rendered. When she met his gaze, his eyes were sympathetic. "It's true then. We really are divorced?"

Harrison's chair squeaked as he leaned back and steepled his fingers. "Yes...and no."

His answer did nothing to slow Alex's racing heart. "I'm confused. We called our lawyer back then. He said he'd take care of it. We were well within Oklahoma's six month waiting period. Why—?"

Harrison held up a hand. "Oklahoma's six-month waiting period is a prohibition on either party getting remarried during that time. It's not a divorce escape clause. Once the paperwork is filed, the divorce is a matter of record. The wording is misleading, but a good attorney would have explained it to you."

Alex shrank into her seat. *Good* attorneys hadn't been in their very limited budgets all those years ago. And there wasn't anything they could do about that either. Nelson

Smith had been in his grave for a decade. Another thing she'd checked on while at the courthouse.

She straightened. "You said yes and no."

The lawyer tapped his pen on his desk. "The original divorce is final, but since you continued to live together as husband and wife, you are considered common-law married under Oklahoma law. If you ever want that to change, you would need to file for a second divorce."

Alex leaned forward in her chair and dropped her head into her hands. Her racing heart had turned into a pounding headache. "Who makes this stuff up?"

Harrison continued, "There's one more thing to consider. Since you guys have never been married to anyone else, you could file paperwork to vacate the divorce."

"I have no clue what that means."

"A couple can choose to vacate...void, if you will...a divorce if they have never been married to anyone else and they decide to get back together. Then they can claim an uninterrupted marriage. It's a good process for couples with joint investments...things like that. It's a simple procedure, one I can initiate for you when you're ready."

"There is nothing simple about this." Alex leaned her head against the back of the chair. "So, I'm divorced...but not really. I'd need a second divorce to walk away from my common-law husband, but you can make it all go away." Alex opened her bag and searched through her things— notes for the church bulletin, new and used tissues, loose change—looking for the old eye shadow container she kept a few pain relievers in. She found it, dumped two into a trembling hand, and chugged them back with a bottle of water.

She closed her eyes and tried to sort through the information. Her irritation with Hunter inched higher with every confusing word the lawyer spoke. Hunter should be with her. The story of her life.

Focus.

OK, she didn't think their congregation would recognize the whole common law thing as a legal marriage, regardless of Hunter's "in the eyes of God" comment from last night. Re-marriage, the sooner, the better, was their only option there. And that vacate thing..."Tell me how that vacate thing works."

Harrison clasped his hands on his desk. "It makes the divorce go away as if it never happened. It's certainly a way to get around the common law issue. You keep the same anniversary date and everything."

Alex pursed her lips. That sounded like something they'd need to do, but even with that, she thought new vows might be in order. Maybe it was a gray area, and she was just overly cautious, but twenty-plus years of divorce—she cringed at the word—needed more than just a piece of paper to make it right.

"How soon can you start the paperwork?" A thought froze her heart. "Will it be in the paper?"

The lawyer frowned at her from across the desk.

"Like marriage licenses, birth announcements...that sort of thing."

"Oh." His expression turned thoughtful. "I've never filed a motion to vacate a divorce. But don't worry, we can make sure it stays private."

"Do we do that before or after we get remarried?"

"As I've said, you guys are legally married as far as the state is concerned and this paperwork—"

"We're pastors, Mr. Lake." Alex reminded him. "We have an organization and a congregation to answer to. If this situation ever sees the light of day, I'm counting on some young-and-stupid leniency"—Alex crossed her fingers in her lap—"being extended by both of those parties. In any case, neither recognizes a common-law marriage as legal. As for the vacate thing...I'll be more comfortable crossing all the T's and dotting the I's."

He nodded. "I sit on the board at Valley View. I think we'd feel the same."

Her eyes went round. "Please don't—"

The lawyer stopped her with an upraised finger. "Lawyer, client confidentiality. No one is going to hear a word of this from me."

She took a breath. *I knew that.* "Thank you. I need to go find my husband and tell him what I've learned while it's still fresh in my mind. We'll get back with you."

"Of course. We can get started as soon as you're ready."

Alex stood, and Harrison Lake came out from behind his desk. "I appreciate you helping me wade through all of this. It's daunting."

He opened his office door. "My pleasure."

Alex stood on the sidewalk in front of the lawyer's office, blinking in the spring sunshine, allowing her eyes to adjust. Her phone rang, and she pulled it from the pocket of her slacks.

"Hello."

"Pastor Alex, did you forget me?"

Alex's shoulders slumped at the sound of Regina Thompson's voice. Between the courthouse and the lawyer, she had, in fact, forgotten her promise to help the youth pastor's wife price items for the garage sale fundraiser. And even more important...she looked at her watch. She had forty-five minutes before a counseling session with bride-to-be Allison Rogers. Hunter was meeting with her fiancé, Eric Varner, before church this evening.

"Hello?"

"Sorry, Regina, I got held up. I'll be there in five minutes." She slipped her phone back into her pocket and kissed the idea of lunch good-bye. Maybe there was a package of peanut butter crackers in the church's pantry. Even though she might be guilty of resenting her absent husband, she loved the ministry and the people of Grace Community as much as he did. Besides, she needed to speak to Hunter, and the church was the most likely place to find him.

THREE HOURS LATER, Alex stood in the open doorway of her husband's office. He was talking on the phone, but he motioned her to a seat and raised a finger, indicating that he was almost done with the call.

"I understand and I'm honored that you'd ask." He paused for a few seconds, his head bobbing in agreement with what he was hearing. "Absolutely. I think a men's retreat is a timely idea. What sort of theme did you have in mind for the sermons?" Another pause. "Building godly families in an ungodly world. That shouldn't be a problem. I can send you some preliminary notes next week, and you can let me know if I'm on the right track." Hunter nodded. "Yes, I have the dates on my calendar. Thanks again for the opportunity."

"What was that all about?" Alex asked when Hunter hung up the phone.

"That was Bishop Maxwell at the district office. The state is putting together a men's retreat for the last week in

June. They're hoping to attract a substantial group in the twenty-five- to fifty-year-old age groups. Two nights of camping under the stars with fishing, target practice, and golf during the day. There's an evening service planned for both nights. If all goes well, they hope to make it an annual event." Hunter sat back, a look of awe on his face. "They've asked me to be the speaker for the inaugural event. Can you believe it?"

Alex smiled at her husband. His lack of attention to anything not church-related might infuriate her at times, but it was hard not to be proud of him, especially when he took everything with such unassuming humility. "Of course I can believe it. You'll be great."

"I appreciate your support, sweetheart. I'll have some juggling to do to keep this in its place. Grace Community and the people here are my first priority." He shook his head. "I don't guess a few more late nights will kill me."

Alex winced at the thought of this new task taking even more of their already compromised time. She met her husband's gaze, wishing she was one of the people who came first in his life. Here it was, nearly three in the afternoon. He hadn't said a word about leaving her to muddle through the mess at the courthouse by herself. Hadn't asked what she'd discovered. She gripped her hands in her lap. She knew exactly what his priorities were...*who* his priorities were. "Everything good with Hazel and her family?"

"She's fine. Just another bout with her dementia. It throws Ed for a loop when his mother forgets who he is."

"I'm sure it's unnerving." Alex waited, hoping Hunter would follow the trail back to their marital issues. When he didn't, she lobbed a grenade in his direction. "I went to the courthouse this morning. The papers the boys gave us are valid. We're divorced...sort of."

Her words hung in the air between them for a couple of heartbeats before Hunter pushed to his feet. He frowned at her as he came around his desk, crossed to the door of the office, and looked up and down the hallway. The door closed with a solid snap, and Hunter twisted the lock. "For heaven's sake, Alexandra. You need to be a little more cautious. What if someone had been outside the door?"

She'd just told him they were divorced, and someone overhearing was the thing that bothered him? Of all the—

He circled back to his seat. "Now, tell me what you found out."

Alex swallowed all of the things hovering on her lips— what good would it do to say them?—and gave him the rundown of all she'd learned, detailing the convoluted and confusing discussion with Harrison Lake. By the time she finished, Hunter sat at his desk with his head in his hands. Alex hoped he was battling half the headache she was.

He looked up and summed it up in a single sentence. "So, we have a divorce we don't want and a marriage recognized by the state but not the organization or the congregation we serve."

"Pretty much," Alex answered.

Hunter blew out a breath. "We need to get remarried as quickly as we can."

"If I understood everything the lawyer said, if we vacate the divorce, we don't have to do anything else. It's like the divorce never happened. We keep our anniversary and everything."

Hunter mulled that. "I think we should still get remarried. It covers all the bases."

Alex leaned forward, excited and gratified that they were on the same page for once. "I was thinking we could take a drive to Branson in the morning. I hear it's lovely in the spring." She paused when she caught the frown on his face. "But you can pick a different place if you like. Give it some thought while you finish up here. I'll go home and pack a couple of bags. We can leave bright and early tomorrow and come home Saturday night all newly married and no one the wiser. You can be back in the pulpit Sunday morning."

Hunter leaned forward on his elbows, and Alex's heart dropped to her toes at the expression of disbelief on his face. "I can't just up and leave town with no notice. Frank Hawkins is in the hospital waiting for a liver transplant. They just placed Millie Ackerman on hospice care. Dane and Mac's babies are due soon." He waved his hand at the phone. "And I have to get some notes ready for Bishop Maxwell."

"But..." Her hands fisted in her lap. "You said yourself that we need to get remarried. I didn't think you'd want to do that here."

"No, here is too risky."

Alex smiled when hope surged.

"But two or three days? That's out of the question. We can run across the state line to Gainesville in the morning, make a stop at their courthouse, and be home by lunchtime. There's no need to take days to do what we can do in a couple of hours."

The words left Alex speechless. How could this be less important to him than the decision about where to get his next hamburger? *How can I be less important?* Alex fought the tears pressing against the back of her eyes. She'd never used them as a weapon, and she refused to start now. "You know, you're right. We don't need to get away for a few days, but what if I want to?" She put her hand over her heart and leaned toward the desk. "What if I want to take this opportunity to reconnect with my husband? Forget want. What if I *need* that time?"

"We've had this conversation, Alex. Healthy churches are not built by part-time ministry."

"And healthy marriages are not built by part-time husbands." Her words were low, issued through clenched teeth. Why couldn't the man ever give her an inch? Just one inch.

Hunter sighed and pulled his calendar closer. He flipped through pages. "Work with me here. Let's do the Gainesville thing tomorrow, and, after I get done with the men's retreat, I'll try to carve out a couple of days to take you on a little getaway, if you still want to go."

A couple of days? Me work with him? Years of neglect and playing second fiddle formed a nasty lump of hurt and resentment in Alex's stomach. Without another word, she picked up her purse and left the office.

"Alex?"

She ignored him and continued down the hall. Her actions were automatic as she got into her car, buckled her seatbelt, and drove toward home.

"Father..." The beginnings of Alex's anguished prayer clogged her throat, and she fought to see the familiar road through the curtain of tears. She discarded prayer and sought to console herself with worn-out bits of self-encouragement. *You know he loves you. He doesn't mean to be insensitive. He doesn't mean to take you for granted. He has a higher calling than just a husband. Choose your battles. You're a pastor's wife—that means sacrifice. Just go along with it, it'll make life easier. What choice do you have...?*

Choices.

The word stopped Alex cold. She had choices, options she hadn't had twenty-four hours ago. The opportunity to fight a twenty-year-old battle in a different way. She pulled into her driveway, turned off the car, and looked at the house she'd called home for so many years. *House and home.* She weighed the words. Yes, the house was warm, dry, and comfortable. It was a big piece of the material blessings God had poured into their lives, but was it really a home? Alex swallowed against the ugly truth scratching at her throat for release.

"Not really." The words were barely a whisper in the private confines of the car. Alex bit her lip as the tears came fresh and hot. *Father...* This time the word was less prayer and more the cry of a distraught child. Dealing with Hunter's neglect had been easier...better...when she'd had the boys to focus on, but since they'd gone off to school, home time was alone time. Time spent rambling around in that house waiting for Hunter to finish the work he loved more than her and come home.

Alex leaned her head against the steering wheel. "Father, I don't think that's the way it's supposed to be. There has to be more to marriage, even a pastor's marriage, than..."—she searched for words and closed her eyes when they came— "loneliness, longing, emptiness." She bit her lip against the final, whispered word, "Bitterness. I love You, I love Hunter, I love the ministry, but I can't live like this. Is this the way you expect me to live?" She shrank from the question and sat silently before her heavenly Father, waiting for an answer.

There was no answer, but neither was there hesitation in her spirit about the step she was about to take. She picked up her cell phone and dialed Jesse's number. She did her best to keep the tears out of her voice when her friend answered.

"Hey, Alex. What's up?"

"Is that apartment over your parents' garage still empty?"

"Sure is. You know someone looking for a place?"

Alex swallowed tears hot enough to scald her throat and gathered the courage to speak the word that would change the course of her life. "Me."

FOUR

Alex pulled clothes from her drawers and linens from the closet and made neat stacks on the end of the bed. Jesse'd assured her that the apartment was furnished. Beyond a bed and a refrigerator Alex had no idea what that meant from a literal perspective, but this house, having sheltered four people, had more sheets and towels than two people could use in a month. Whatever she decided to take, Hunter wouldn't miss.

Will I need dishes and pans? What about my books?

Alex sank onto the edge of the bed and put her head in her hands. This was too hard. *Father, am I being unreasonable?* The question brought no more response now than it had earlier. No release to go, no injunction to stay. Alex rubbed her hands on her denim-clad thighs as she straightened. *I guess, sometimes, you have to do what you have to do.*

She pulled her luggage out of the closet, laid the pieces out on the floor, and piled stuff in. She'd take her clothes and toiletries, box up a few necessities from the kitchen, throw in a few books and her laptop, and call it good. She could always come back for more. It wasn't as if she were leaving town, or even avoiding Hunter. She just needed some space, in a neutral place, to work out the conflicting emotions in her heart.

Besides, now that she knew the divorce was legal, she didn't feel right staying here with Hunter. They needed to remarry. *There's no need to take days to do what we can do in a couple of hours.* Hunter's words rang in Alex's ears, every word true. It wasn't the words Alex took exception to, but the attitude behind them. His never-changing assertion, intentional or not, that she wasn't worth his time, that out of the five hundred members of his congregation, she was no more than the five hundredth.

She zipped up the two large bags, rolled them down the tiled floor of the hall, and parked them next to the front door. The doorbell rang just as she turned for the kitchen. Alex peeked out the side window. Her heart dropped with dread and swelled with love at the same time. Her friends crowded the porch. Charley in her uniform, thumbs tucked into the wide shiny leather of her utility belt. Mac, one hand braced against the small of her back, leaning, just a little, on Jesse. Randy and Syd, one blonde, one redheaded, still dressed in their business attire, obviously fresh from the bank.

Alex leaned her head against the door and breathed a prayer. *Father, I'm so glad to see them. But...they can't be here.* The conflicting statements shredded her heart, and, for the first time since coming to Garfield, Alex knew what it was to have her support system ripped out from under her. She'd held these women up and loved them through some of the toughest times of their lives, would again if the situation called for it. But in the last twenty-four hours the foundation of her world had cracked, and she couldn't share it with them. Her friends were members of Hunter's congregation, and there wasn't a thing she could tell them without violating the trust of that position.

The bell rang a second time. Alex dashed at the tears on her face and pulled the door open. "Girls, I can't...you can't..." The tears came harder, stealing her ability to speak. She took a step back, prepared to close the door. Five bodies inserted themselves into the opening.

"That's not going to happen," Randy said.

"But I—"

"You don't have to tell us what's going on," Randy continued.

"Not a single word," Charley agreed. "The fact that you're hurting is all we need to know."

"You need us, and we're here," Jesse said. "We don't have to know why."

Alex blinked her eyes and frowned when she saw a sixth woman coming up the walk. What was Lisa Sisko doing here?

Lisa lifted a finger to her lips as she came up behind the other women.

"Jesse called us," Mac said. "We brought some things for the apartment."

"And we want to pray with you," Syd said.

"That's a marvelous idea." Lisa shouldered her way to the front of the group. "Why don't we move this into the house?" She put an arm around Alex and steered her into the living room. The others hesitated for just a second before they followed. Syd came in last and closed the door.

Lisa pulled Alex into a hug and spoke into her ear. "Do you trust me?"

Alex nodded, closed her eyes, and sank into the embrace of friendship. She felt Lisa raise her head.

"You guys are a treasure," Lisa said. "Gather round. Let's bring our friend to her Father's attention."

There was a second or so of shuffling, and Alex felt hands on her back, arms, and shoulders. Alex wept hot tears onto Lisa's shoulder. *Thank you, Father. I need You, and them, so much.*

"Jesus," Lisa began, "we need Your presence in this place. You have strength for us when we're weary. You have shelter for us when we're overwhelmed. You have answers for us when everything we know is called into question. You have healing for a heart shattered into pieces beneath our feet. We're grateful that You are these things for us each and every day. Father, You love Alex above and beyond the present situation. Remind her of that right now. Lift her up and help her find her place as Your child. Calm the storm in her life and bring her a sure and true direction as she moves forward. We ask these things in the confidence of Your love and in Jesus' name."

LISA LIFTED her head and studied the women huddled around them. She'd met them, worked closely with them while planning Alex's women's conference. An event that had gone off without a hitch just two weeks ago. Each of the women wore tears on their faces. Each one would have to trust her with their friend. *Father, give me the right words here.*

As the women began to take a step back and swipe at their wet cheeks, Lisa took a firmer hold on Alex and let her gaze travel from face to face. "Guys, we've worked together a little bit, but I know you don't know me well." She smiled at Mac. "Well, most of you don't." Lisa drew in a deep breath.

"The fact that you're here tells me so much about you and the love you have for your pastor's wife...your friend. She's blessed to have you, but having you is a hard thing for her right now."

Jesse nodded. "We know. We just want to help."

"I know that. I'm going to ask you to do something you don't want to do. I'm going to ask you to trust me with your friend."

Mac put both hands on the small of her back and did a tiny backwards stretch. Lisa bit her lip to keep an amused smile from her face. Like Alex, Lisa had carried twins and knew the sacrifice it took to be any place except a recliner this close to her due date.

There was an audible pop as the kink in Mac's back released. She straightened with a sigh. "What do you mean?"

"I heard most of what you said out on the porch. Alex is your pastor's wife. There's a code of conduct there that she can't break. It's obvious that you respect that, even though it might sting your hearts. That doesn't mean that you can't help her, it just means that your help will have to take a different form than the confidences I'm sure you've shared in the past. Pray for her, take her to lunch, cook a meal for her, but let me be the one she confides in for now."

The other five women looked at each other. "She's been a rock for us," the redheaded Randy said.

The cop frowned. "I've known her since college." She held up a hand to stop Lisa's answering comment. "But I know this is best for her."

"As long as she knows we're not leaving because we don't love her," Syd said.

Lisa squeezed Alex. "Girlfriend, you are blessed right down to your toenails."

Alex drew in a shuddering breath, untangled herself from Lisa's arms, and faced her friends. There were black streaks on her cheeks from her ruined mascara, and Lisa was glad for her navy blue blouse that wouldn't show the stains.

"I love you guys so much, but Lisa's right. I need to talk and I"—her voice cracked with fresh tears— "I can't share this with you. Even if you'd take it to your graves if I asked, I just can't."

Jesse took a small step forward. "Then give us something we can do."

"You guys brought stuff for the apartment?" Alex asked.

Five nods answered her question.

"You're the best. Can you take it over there for me while I visit with Lisa?"

"If that's what you need us to do," Randy said.

Alex closed her eyes. "That's what I need. If you want to wait for me there, I shouldn't be long. You can help me settle in."

Lisa motioned to the suitcases next to the door. "Why don't y'all take those along with you? That way Alex won't have to wrestle them around by herself." She kept an arm around Alex as the women moved toward the door. She waited until the last one left before she shifted to take Alex's hand and lead her to the sofa. "God woke us up out of a sound sleep last night to pray for you and Hunter." She sat and patted the cushion beside her. "Talk to me."

ALEX WAS TOO WIRED to sit. Instead, she tugged her

hand free, moved back to the window, and watched as, one by one, her friends got into their cars and pulled away from the curb. "Thanks for that," she whispered to Lisa. "Sending them away when everything in me needs them might have been more than I could have managed."

"They're a great group of women," Lisa said. "It must be hard not to lean on them the way they've leaned on you, but I think they get it."

The calm words sent fresh tears to Alex's eyes, and she turned away, twisting her hands at her waist. "It stinks that they have to, don't you think?"

"No one ever said that being called to be a pastor's wife was easy."

Emotions flip-flopped in Alex's stomach. Resentment at being denied the luxury of her inner circle crowded her and rolled into the already ugly mess her emotions had become since leaving the church. "God made me a woman a long time before he made me a pastor's wife." She reached out and straightened the edge of one of the sheer, blue curtains. "And now I'm not even that." The whispered words hung in the silence of the house. Alex lifted her hands to her face and wept into them. "I don't know what to do."

"I think this is where I came in." Lisa rose, put an arm around Alex's shoulder, and steered her to the sofa. "You can talk it out with me, woman to woman...pastor's wife to pastor's wife. I'll listen, and we'll pray." She dug a crumpled tissue from the pocket of her shirt and shook it open. "Here you go, it's clean. Now, spill it. What's got you packing your bags?"

Alex mopped her face and stared at the floor for a few seconds. Instead of answering Lisa's question, she looked into her friend's face and asked one of her own. "If you could change one thing in your life, what would it be?"

Lisa sat back, visibly mystified. "That's an intriguing question." She stared across the room for a couple of heartbeats. "Well, there are the obvious, knee-jerk answers. I could say that I wish I'd had a more attentive father, but in all honesty, his neglect shaped me into the person I am, so maybe not. I might wish away that horrible tornado that trapped me and Dave in a closet for a few hours, but that's what ultimately brought us together and brought us to Garfield, so I guess I have to leave that alone too. We lost our home in a house fire at Christmastime eight years ago, but that led to the dream house we live in now." She shrugged. "I got nothing. The big things impact too much of my life, and the little things aren't worth the trouble of rearview angst. Why?"

"Because I've been given the biggest do-over in my life. And I'm not sure what I should do with it."

"OK."

Alex shoved up from the sofa, pacing a circuit around the room while she told Lisa about the unexpected news her sons had delivered the night before. She detailed her solitary trip to the courthouse and her visit with the lawyer. Her voice cracked, and fresh tears ran down her cheeks as she related Hunter's just-get-it-over-with, I'm-too-busy-to-give-you-my-time attitude.

Alex stopped in front of Lisa. "And the sprinkles on the cupcake of my day? I can't go to the people I'd trust with my life for advice and comfort." She stopped and bit her lip. "I'm sorry for the way that sounded. I love you and I appreciate your being here for me, but I guess...it just hit me, all at once today, that the ministry hasn't only cost me my marriage, it's cost me my friends too." She whirled away. "And to hear those words come out of my mouth when there's nothing in this world I love more than Jesus..." She crossed her arms around herself and wept. *Oh, Father, I'm so sorry and so confused.*

"Come sit." Lisa waited for Alex to join her. "In the first place, you don't have to apologize to me. I know exactly what you mean. As far as your friends are concerned, they respect you as much as they love you. I don't think you have anything to worry about there. That was a pretty determined group of ladies we just sent away. I think you're gonna find some new depth there before this is over."

Lisa took Alex's hands and pulled in a deep breath. "It's your marriage that's the most important thing right now. I have intimate knowledge of where you are. My father was a powerful man of God, but when it came to his family, he didn't have a clue. A minister has to walk a fine line between his ministry and his marriage, but think about this. Long before there was a minister, God made Adam a husband. Marriage was the first institution that God blessed."

Alex tilted her head. "I never thought about it that way."

"I have," Lisa said. "I wasn't marrying Dave and raising a family in the same sort of neglect I endured. Dave and I had years of counseling, before and after we married, to learn how to safeguard our marriage. It's a constant work in progress, and sometimes that line gets crossed, but as ministers, it's up to us to be doubly careful about building a wall around our home and families. How can we lead our congregations toward solid, healthy marriages if we don't have one ourselves?"

"Exactly." Alex bowed her head and stared at her folded hands, turning her friend's words over and over, looking for a catch and finding hope. "So what should I do?

I mean...how do Hunter and I get from where we are to where you guys are?"

Lisa smiled. "You don't get to *our* place, you get to find your *own* place. And I can't tell you how to do that, but if you can answer some questions, I think we can find the right direction."

Alex sat straight. "OK."

"Do you love Hunter?"

Alex's answer was immediate. "With all my heart."

"Do you think Hunter loves you?"

This time the answer was a little slower to come. "I guess so...I mean...I hope so?"

Lisa stared at her.

Alex let out a deep breath. "Probably, but I don't think he knows how to show it."

"We'll count that as a yes," Lisa said. "OK, you love each other. That's a foundation we can build on." This time it was Lisa's turn to pace. "This whole divorce-marriage thing you guys have going on is just messed up, but I agree with you on the remarriage thing. That needs to happen as soon as possible. Is it safe to say that that isn't an option under the current circumstances?"

Alex leaned forward, her elbows on her knees, her head on her fisted hands. "That's just it, Lisa. I haven't felt like I was part of a real marriage in so long, I can't even remember what that's like. Despite what a younger version of me wanted, I don't think I'd have considered a divorce. But, now that it's done..." She looked up. "It gives me some options."

"What do you mean?"

"For the first time in twenty-plus years, I'm in a position to make Hunter see how I feel. I don't...I don't mean that I want to punish him, but if there's a way to make what we have better...stronger...even if that means a time of separation while we work towards that, that's got to be a good thing."

"Sounds like you're talking about a controlled separation."

"I guess, maybe. That's a real thing?"

Lisa laughed. "Yes, it's a real thing. You can Google it and everything. It works when both parties are committed to seeing the marriage work out in the end. You work with a counselor—"

"That's going to be a problem for Hunter. He wants to keep this whole divorce thing quiet."

"Will he talk to Dave?"

"Probably..." Alex drew the word out, hesitant to speak for her husband.

"Problem solved, then," Lisa said. "Because I know for a fact that Dave will be talking to Hunter before the day is over. Like I said, God woke us both up last night with a burden for you guys."

"Thank you."

Lisa waved the gratitude away. "In a controlled separation, the couple lives apart while working with a set of specific guidelines designed to bring their marriage back into harmony."

"Like...?"

"Just things like you'd both agree not to file for divorce during the process." Lisa grinned at her friend. "Not an issue here, I guess. Maybe a time limit on your time apart, and an agreement on when and where you plan to see each other. Will there be intimacy, how will your finances be handled? The most important thing is that it gives you both some space to breathe, a chance to see each other in a new light, to reconnect with the things that made you fall in love in the first place while you work on the things that are driving you apart."

Despite the dismal situation, optimism stirred in Alex's heart. "What do I need to do to get started?"

Lisa took her seat next to Alex and held her hands. "First we pray." She closed her eyes, and Alex did the same. "Father, this is a difficult and unusual situation, but You are not surprised. Alex wants Your perfect direction for her life and Hunter's."

Alex squeezed her friend's hands when her heart twisted. *Oh, Father, You know I do.*

"She loves You and her husband. She's looking to You for healing in her marriage and a clear path for the future. Shelter the twins during this challenging time. Help them offer loving support to both of their parents. Do a work in Hunter's heart as well. He knows Your voice, but there's a truth to marriage he's overlooked. Help him find his way. And Father, Dave and I need your special wisdom as we love and counsel our friends. We ask these things in Your name, Jesus."

Lisa looked up. "Now, go move into that apartment and spend a few minutes with your friends. We'll work forward from there."

FIVE

Hunter unlocked the front door after service Wednesday evening, pushed it open, and stepped inside. There was no light left on to greet him. No aroma from a meal warming in the microwave welcomed him. No Alex coming down the hall or looking up from her place on the sofa where she read to ask him about his day. None of those things existed in his world tonight because Alex had left him.

"She left me." Even whispered aloud, the words made no sense, but she was gone.

Without explanation.

Well, not a reasonable one, as far as he was concerned. They needed to fix this divorce thing. They agreed on that. He'd laid out a perfectly good plan. It wasn't what Alex wanted, but it got the job done quietly with no fuss. But no. Instead of a discreet marriage tomorrow, he'd gotten a phone call this afternoon. Alex was *tired of being last on his priority list. She deserved more than the leftover hours of his day.* Nothing new there. Well, except for her final ultimatum. There would be no remarriage until they'd addressed the problems in their relationship.

As if he had time for that. Hunter was a busy pastor shepherding almost five hundred people. Those people had needs, and God had called him to help meet those needs. He didn't have time for marital temper tantrums.

Sometimes you have to leave the four hundred ninety-nine and go after the one.

Hunter pushed the thought aside. He chased down church stragglers every day of his life. His wife shouldn't be one of them. He pushed the door closed, hard, flinching when the sound echoed like a shot.

He looked at his watch. Alex had also informed him that he could expect a visit and an explanation from Dave Sisko this evening. Though what Dave had to do with this, Hunter couldn't fathom. And oh, one more thing...she'd moved into an apartment over Walter and Mavis Cooper's garage for the time being. He ran a hand through his hair. Perfect...just perfect. Walter and Mavis were members of his church. Mavis was one of the most opinionated, nosy... Hunter scrubbed his hands down his face. So much for keeping their private issues private. This whole thing was beyond his comprehension.

Problems? Every relationship had problems. You didn't solve problems by running away. You solved them by staying and working through them. Hadn't they counseled hundreds of couples over the course of their ministry? In the absence of abuse, not a single time had they recommended any sort of separation. Why did she think that was the proper course now?

"She left me." He whispered the words a second time. The silence of the house swallowed them up without a trace.

"Fine." Hunter dropped his keys into the dish on the table next to the door. His purposeful stride carried him to the kitchen. He could fend for himself for a couple of days. He knew how to open a can of soup and make a sandwich. Forget the fact that he'd worked all day on nothing but a fast food breakfast biscuit and a half wilted salad he'd purchased during one of his hospital visits. It wasn't as if he deserved a pleasant voice and a hot meal at the end of a long day.

He yanked open the cabinet, stooped down to study his choices, and snatched out a can of loaded potato soup. He kicked the door closed and smacked the can down on the countertop. The slamming of the door and the bang of the can reverberated in the quiet house. Hunter stared at the can as if it were the culprit.

He leaned on the counter and took a series of deep breaths. He needed to lose some of the anger before Dave Sisko arrived. Dave was eight years his junior and, though they were members of different church organizations, they enjoyed a solid friendship. Hunter had become something of a mentor to the younger man since old Pastor Gordon and his wife had retired and moved to Houston to be closer to their family. It wouldn't do for Dave to see him so worked up.

While the soup warmed in the microwave, Hunter dug through the refrigerator for ham, cheese, lettuce, and tomato. He slapped a thin plastic cutting board onto the counter, grabbed a knife from the block next to the sink, and attacked the tomato with the fervor of an Israelite priest preparing an ox for a burnt sacrifice. The knife clattered to the counter when his clumsy effort cut through more than the stubborn skin of the tomato. Blood welled across the top of his finger. He reached for it with his tomato juice soaked right hand, eyes widening when the vegetable's acid seeped into the cut. He scrambled for the sink, turned the cold water on full, and shoved both hands under the flow. The water stung and cooled at the same time. Hunter studied the cut. It bled freely, but it didn't appear to be deep or life-threatening.

He shook his right hand dry and reached for the paper towel rack. He yanked one free just as the doorbell rang. So much for getting dinner done before his visitor arrived. Hunter wrapped his injured finger, nudged the faucet closed, and retraced his steps to the front door.

He pulled the door open and stepped back. As expected, Dave Sisko stood framed in the opening. Dave grinned then frowned as his eyes traveled downward. "What did you do?"

Hunter jerked his injured hand up. Even wrapped, gravity had done its job on the wound. Blood stained the paper towel, and when he looked down the hall, he saw that small drops of blood had marked his path. "Stupid!"

Dave raised an eyebrow and took a step back.

"Not you." Hunter almost smiled as he turned back to the kitchen and motioned Dave to follow. "Come on in. Alex has a first aid kit under the sink. If I can stop the bleeding, I'll make us both a sandwich."

DAVE FOLLOWED Hunter into the kitchen. He cut around the older man and pointed to a chair. "Sit. I'll doctor you up, and then *I'll* make the sandwiches. I'm not overly fond of blood as a condiment."

"Funny."

Dave stooped and looked into the cavernous space under the sink. His gaze fell on a small white box with a red cross stenciled on the top. "Here we go." He pulled it free, wet a second paper towel, and turned to the table. Hunter had his finger unwrapped, and blood dripped slowly to puddle onto the paper towel beneath it.

"What did you do?"

Hunter lifted his chin in the direction of the cutting board.

Dave took in the half sliced tomato, the knife five times too big for the job, and the blood-and-juice dotted cutting board. "Hmm..." He pulled out a chair next to Hunter, opened the box, and studied the contents. "Let's see what we have for a tomato killer."

"Your bedside manner stinks."

Dave rummaged through bandages, gauze, ointments, and tweezers. "Here we go." He pulled out a small bottle and unscrewed the top. "This will fix you up. Give me your hand."

"What is it?"

"It's a liquid bandage. Lisa uses it on the kids. It seals and medicates in one step."

Hunter grunted but offered the injury to Dave.

Dave was happy to see the cut clotting. "It's definitely a bleeder, but it's not too deep." He cleaned the cut with the fresh paper towel, held Hunter's hand firmly, and dabbed the spot with the little brush.

Hunter pulled in a sharp breath. "Holy..."

Dave resisted his friend's attempt to jerk his hand away. "What are you, five? Hold still."

Hunter exhaled slowly. "Stings worse than the tomato juice."

"I said it was effective. I didn't say it was painless."

"Lisa uses this on the kids?"

Dave grinned. "When she can catch them." He leaned over and blew a breath across the cut. "There, there, little man. Uncle Dave has you all fixed up."

"Not funny." Hunter jerked his hand free and examined the wound.

Dave leaned back in his chair. "You can expect my bill later in the week." He pushed back from the table and gathered up the first aid supplies and the bloody paper towels. He put a hand on Hunter's shoulder when he started to stand. "Just sit. I meant it, I'll finish the sandwiches." He picked up the chef's knife with the wicked-looking blade. "Really? It was a tomato, for crying out loud. Talk about overkill." Dave turned on the water and held the knife under the steaming hot stream before wiping it dry and putting it back in the block. He looked over the choices and selected a medium-sized paring knife with a serrated edge. He held it up for Hunter's inspection. "A much better option and a whole lot less deadly."

"Whatever." Hunter sat back in the chair and crossed his arms. "There's a bowl of soup in the microwave. It probably needs a couple more minutes. You'll find another bowl in the cabinet to your left."

Dave reached out and pushed a few buttons on the microwave before going back to building sandwiches. "Thanks anyway. I'm not a big fan of soup." It had been a staple of the orphanage he'd grown up in, and he'd never found much taste for it as an adult. Five minutes later they faced each other from opposite sides of the table. Hunter's soup sent up a cloud of fragrant steam, and Dave had constructed three sandwiches with no further bloodshed. One for Hunter and two for himself.

"I'll bless it, if you like," Dave offered. He bowed his head when Hunter answered with a nod. "Father, thank You for the food You've provided for us this evening. Please bless it and our conversation. Give us calm and focused minds and an understanding of Your will. Amen."

"AMEN," Hunter muttered before picking up his spoon. Dave's prayer had been both a blessing and a reminder of the younger man's purpose here. They'd traded barbs about the cut and food preparation, but Dave's visit wasn't a joke or a social call. The reminder threatened to rob Hunter of his appetite. He took a deep breath and focused on his bowl, determined that if Dave had something to say about Alex's defection, he'd have to be the one to bring it up.

The food disappeared while the silence stretched. Dave had half a sandwich left, and Hunter watched as the younger man toyed with his food. Good. Hunter wasn't in the mood to discuss his wife, so Dave could just keep his thoughts... Hunter frowned when Dave pushed his plate to the side.

"We can dance around this all night, but you know why I'm here. Ignoring it won't make it go away."

"Alex."

Dave nodded. "Yes, but more than that. I need to tell you that God woke Lisa and me up last night and told us to pray for you guys. We had no idea why, but He was pretty insistent." He held up a hand when Hunter opened his mouth to explain. "Lisa spent part of the day with Alex. We've talked. I know about the divorce."

"Then you know she left me."

"I do know that." Dave studied him from across the table. "In an effort to be transparent to both of you, I need to tell you that I had a long visit with Alex today in my office. I want you to know that I'm not here because I'm on her side. You also need to understand that I won't automatically be on yours. I'm here to act as a Christian counselor and to help explain what Alex's moving out means, and what she hopes to gain."

Hunter sat back. "She couldn't tell me those things herself?" He raised his hands. "I've never failed to listen to my wife when she had a problem. Why should this be any different?"

Across the table, Dave bowed his head, and Hunter saw his lips moving in what he took as a silent prayer. When his head came up, Hunter frowned at the look of determination on the younger man's face.

Dave braced his arms on the table and leaned forward. "I've no doubt that you listen. But, do you address her concerns with anything more than lip service?"

The quiet question knocked Hunter back and turned him defensive. "Lip service? I've been a faithful husband and a dependable provider for more than twenty years. I've given my wife a comfortable home, financial security, and the luxury of raising our family as a stay-at-home mother. Not once in our marriage has she had to worry about where I am and what I'm doing." He mirrored Dave's leaned-in pose. "I understand that she has some issues with my work and the time it takes, but she has the things I just mentioned because of that work and God's blessing on it. What more can I possibly give her?"

Dave met his gaze. "Time." The word fell from his lips and hung between them. Hunter closed his eyes. If time was the element that would save his marriage, then he and Alex were doomed. He looked at his friend and held his hands open in surrender. "Time has never been mine to give."

SIX

Alex glanced at the clock above the stove in her new apartment's tiny kitchen. It was inching toward nine p.m. *What was taking so long?* She circled her fingertip around the top of her tea glass and tried to imagine the conversation happening across town between Hunter and Dave. *Hunter wouldn't dismiss her demands out of hand, would he?* She bit her lip and tried to bolster her frazzled nerves. *Don't borrow trouble. He'll listen. He has to.*

I hope.

But this was new ground. Hunter as the counseled instead of the counselor. Would he take his frustrations out on Dave? *Father, this is the first day of what could be a lengthy process. You know my heart. Help us both to have open hearts and minds. Help us find Your will for our future.* She scooted away from the bar, stood, and paced to the window. "Dave should have called by now, don't you think?"

"Calm down," Lisa said. "He'll call once they've talked. You told Dave that Hunter likely wouldn't get home until eight, later if something at the church needed his attention. They're probably just getting started."

Something at the church always needs Hunter's attention. The thought carried an underlying bitterness that Alex was ashamed to own much less voice. Instead she turned back to her friend with a smile of gratitude. "I appreciate your being here, but you don't have to hold my hand. You should go home. The kids—"

"The kids are just fine. Alex babysits her brothers. Well, maybe babysitting is a poor choice of words, since Jared and Jordon are eleven and pretty self-sufficient. It's how she earns extra money."

"Your Alex is growing into a lovely young lady. She's thirteen now, right?"

"Thirteen going on thirty."

Alex laughed. "I guess that's pretty normal with girls. Boys don't seem to grow up quite so fast." She returned to the bar and sipped her iced tea. The cold liquid felt good on her parched throat. "It's great that she's willing to lend a hand. You're very blessed. I always wanted a girl."

"Then why did you stop with the boys?" Lisa asked. "I mean, twins can be a challenge, but it's not so bad if you space them out a bit."

"I always wanted a big family," Alex said, "but God had a different plan. Sean and Benjamin came at seven months. A hard labor that turned into a C-section delivery that resulted in a hysterectomy. We weren't sure either of the boys would make it through that first week, they were so small, and their little lungs weren't quite ready for the outside world. When they finally turned the corner and started to thrive, we were so grateful for the blessing of two healthy boys, it was hard to worry about what we might miss out on down the road."

"You could have adopted."

"I thought of it once or twice over the years, but I never brought it up. By the time the boys started school..." Alex's words faded as her mind drifted to the years when she'd functioned as a single parent, forced to juggle activities on her own that should have been shared with their father. Football for Sean, baseball for Benjamin, track for both. Bible quiz, talent shows, and guitar lessons, Boy Scouts, fights in middle school, broken hearts in high school. Maybe God knew what He was doing after all. How would she have handled it for three kids...or more?

"By the time the boys started school, what?" Lisa asked.

Alex shook herself out of the avalanche of memories. "Nothing. I was just thinking that I feel bad that you guys are spending time with us that should be spent with your family."

Lisa cocked her head and studied her friend. "It's not an issue, but it is a great object lesson."

"How so?"

"Just that ministry is a people-oriented vocation and very fluid. No matter what you and Hunter work out together, no matter how many walls you build around your marriage, there will still be times when a legitimate emergency forces a compromise. You want Hunter to see your side of this argument. You have to be prepared to see his."

———

NOT HIS TO GIVE? Dave stared at the older man. "You're going to have to explain that one."

"Explain what?" Hunter asked. "You and I are both leading growing congregations. That takes time. Time I dedicated to God the moment I said yes to His call to the ministry. Alex has always stood by my side, but I don't think she's ever quite understood what's mine and what isn't."

Dave propped his elbow on the table and rested his chin on his hand. "Hmm. Take me through a normal day."

Hunter stared at him, but complied. "I start my day in the office at eight. The mornings are reserved for administrative tasks. All of the department heads at Grace Community know that if they have problems they need to discuss, they can find me there until eleven. I generally head out to make hospital visits next. That usually takes two to three hours, given the travel time to and from. I eat lunch while I'm out. Most days I make it back to my office by two. I have mid-week and Sunday sermons to prepare for, so my prayer and study time is until six. If I have any counseling scheduled, it's from six on." Hunter shrugged. "That's the plan I shoot for. If there's an emergency, then the schedule goes out the window, and things get rearranged as necessary."

Dave pulled a small notebook from his pocket and jotted a few notes. "That's twelve hours. You maintain this schedule every day?"

"Of course," Hunter answered. "You don't?"

Dave snapped the notebook shut. "No, I don't. I'm not Moses. Neither are you."

"I beg your pardon?"

"Moses, Hunter, you remember Moses? He's the guy who went out every day to sit at court with all of the people of Israel. When his father-in-law saw what was going on, he told Moses that he was going to wear himself out. That he should delegate some of the easier tasks to godly men. If you want a New Testament reference to the same principle, reread Acts, chapter six. The disciples couldn't be all things to all people. You can't either."

"So your advice to me is to sacrifice the needs of my

congregation in favor of the needs of my personal life?" Hunter's expression hardened. "I won't...I can't...do that."

Dave sat back in his chair and studied his friend. "I'm not telling you how to run your ministry. I'm just making a Father Jethro suggestion." He propped his elbow on the table and balanced his chin on his fist. He thought for a few seconds before he straightened with a smile. "You have youth and children's pastors, but have you ever thought about adding an assistant minister to your staff?"

Hunter frowned at the suggestion. "To do what?"

"Lots of things. Let him fill the pulpit one Sunday a month. Give him responsibility for the mid-week sermons. If not all of them, you could alternate months with him. He could do a lot of the hospital visitation—"

"My people like to know I'm there for them."

"And you should be," Dave agreed. "When someone is newly admitted, when someone is having surgery, people want their pastor. But, the day after someone has a baby... the day after surgery, if all is well, an assistant would be a second friendly face, a second person praying. He could even do some of the counseling." Dave paused when he saw Hunter's frown deepen.

"I can tell you don't like that idea, but let me give you an example. Do you have any experience dealing with alcoholism? Not people you've counseled but real-life experience?" He continued when Hunter shook his head. "What if the assistant minister you hire had been raised by alcoholic parents? His understanding of the situation would bring a whole new dimension to that counseling session that you couldn't hope to duplicate." Dave grinned. "I'm not saying that you should look for that, but I think you get the idea. We all have valuable life experiences."

Hunter picked at the clear patch of bandage on his finger. "I don't know."

"I'm not suggesting that you make these decisions tonight, but I do think you need to start praying about them. And I think Moses is a great example for this situation. He was a godly man hard at work, spending his days at the "church," doing his best to do what God called him to do. But it doesn't look as if he'd asked God's direction about dealing with the day-to-day task of ministry. He just got in the habit of doing it all on his own. He never thought of an alternative until Jethro suggested it.

"Beyond delegation there are a few practical things you can do to open up some time for your wife. I know you have a nice home office. Invest in a laptop that can travel with you and work on some of that "administrative" stuff at home. Invite Alex in for a shared cup of coffee when the work is caught up, or, better yet, linger over breakfast before you get busy. If someone really needs you, you can be at the church in five minutes. Take the time to share your visitation schedule with her. If she has errands nearby, offer to meet her for lunch. Shuffle your counseling appointments so that you can be home, and work-free, by six two or three nights a week. All of these things will go a long way toward healing the neglect—"

"Neglect?" Hunter bristled. "My family is not neglected. I've worked hard to make sure that they are well provided for."

Dave held his ground. "Provision is not attention, Hunter. You object to the word neglect. Do you prefer the word abuse?"

Hunter's face went red. "I've never laid a hand—"

"Abuse isn't always physical." Dave shot back. "I know you can quote me scripture and verse about the responsibilities of a minister, but I can give you just as many about the responsibilities of a husband and father. Psalm 128:3 says that your wife should be like a fruitful vine. A fruitful vine needs cultivation. Cultivation requires the time and attention of the vinedresser. First Peter 3:7 instructs us to dwell with our wives according to knowledge, giving honor to them as the weaker vessel. God ordained some men to be husbands and some to be ministers. For some, like you and me, He ordained both roles. It's up to us to take a step back and see where the line in the middle is. You might have some trouble seeing it at first, but it's there."

Dave paused to let his words soak in. He couldn't tell by the enigmatic look on Hunter's face if the man was considering what he'd said or considering throwing him out the door. When Hunter said nothing, Dave said, "Can I ask you a question?"

The older man nodded.

"If a member of your congregation came to you and told you that their family was suffering because their spouse was spending twelve to fourteen hours a day working—not because they needed the money, not because their job depended on it, but just because of a personal choice—what would you do?"

Hunter scrubbed both of his hands down his face before facing Dave. "I'd do what I could to help the offending spouse see what his choices were costing him."

"Exactly." Dave tapped the table. "What have your choices cost you today, my friend?"

Hunter's sigh filled the room. "OK, I've got some things to pray about and some things to work on. But, even if God tells me to change my direction, these things are not going to correct themselves in a week. Alex needs to come home so we can fix the legalities of our marriage and work on the rest. My congregation—"

"That's what you're worried about? What your congregation thinks?"

Hunter stared at him.

"I hate to break this to you, but that's a problem. In fact, if your congregation is your biggest worry, then your wife has a point."

Hunter sat back, crossed his arms. But he didn't argue.

"Pulling your marriage back together is going to take work," Dave said. "Long, hard, focused, visible work. If your congregation sees your humanity in the middle of this battle, then so be it. Ministers are people too. We bleed, we cry, we have problems. The good ones strive to deal with them in a Biblically-sanctioned fashion. Let your people see your humanity. Your humility. Let them learn from your struggle. Let them see you constructing some walls around your marriage. You're acting on the same advice you'd give any one of them. How is that a bad thing?"

Hunter rubbed his temples. "There's no reason we can't do that under the same roof."

"Alex seems to disagree with you on that. But hey"—he pulled folded papers from his pocket— "you'll have plenty of time to try to make her see it your way." He spread the documents on the table.

Hunter regarded them suspiciously. "What's all that?"

"The guidelines for a controlled separation and Alex's suggestions. We'll go over them. I'll take your input back to her. Once everything is agreed upon, you'll both get a copy of the completed and signed agreement."

Hunter pulled the pages close and leaned over them, muttering as he read. "Time limit for the separation, six weeks." He looked up at Dave. "I'm not living like this for a month and a half. Four weeks. That's my *input.*" The last word carried more than a little sarcasm.

Dave slid a pen across the table. "Make a note."

Hunter scribbled and continued reading. "Counseling once a week." He shook his head but moved to the next points. "Money to cover her living expenses." Hunter looked up. "Seriously? What does she think I'm going to do, cut her off without a penny?"

"It's the standard language. I don't think she meant anything negative by it."

"Whatever," he mumbled before moving to the next page. "So she plans to attend service as normal?"

Dave nodded. "Neither of you have done anything wrong. Alex understands the importance of presenting a united front to your congregation."

Hunter blew out an impatient breath and continued to read. A frown clouded his expression, and he tapped the final point. "What's this?"

Dave turned the papers so he could see. "Starting next week, she would like to have dinner together two evenings a week during the separation period. Alex will cook one of those meals, you are responsible for planning the second. At least six to nine both nights. Marital issues will not be discussed during these evening visits. This is time for you guys to try to reconnect with the things that attracted you to each other in the first place." He looked up. "That's all pretty self-explanatory. What needs clarification?"

Hunter sat back. "Two evenings a week? I just...I mean..." He shrugged, obviously at a loss. "I didn't think we'd start with so...much..." His words trailed off as Dave gave him an incredulous stare.

"Hunter, there are one hundred and sixty-eight hours in a week and you're balking about spending six of them with your wife?" He paused, waiting for his friend to make some sort of redeeming comment.

Nothing came.

He gathered the papers, tapped them together, and slipped them back into his pocket. "We've definitely got our work cut out for us."

SEVEN

Alex sat at her tiny bar with her second cup of coffee on Thursday morning, two herculean tasks complete. Job one had been an early call to Sean and Benjamin. They needed to know about the authenticity of that stupid divorce decree and her decision to move out of the family home until things could be resolved. She'd wrestled with the *how to* all night long, abhorring the phone call, but worried that they might hear it from a friend first if she didn't make the call.

Their reactions had been true to their individual dispositions. Benjamin, being the more pragmatic and outspoken, had jumped to her defense, angry with his father, and determined to ditch his classes to come spend the day with her. Sean, the quieter one, had offered the same but with less vehemence and asked how his father was handling the situation. She'd met the challenge of keeping them in school for the day with assurances that she was fine and that both she and their father were seeking counseling to restore their marriage. She offered to fix dinner for the both of them.

"I'll explain all of the details in person." An answer to Benjamin's question.

"No, Dad won't be here." That for Sean.

"Yes, we can have lasagna." Though Benjamin had lobbed that one out, Sean had jumped on the lasagna-train.

The end of the call brought Alex to job two. Her first cooking-for-one, mostly, grocery list in more than twenty years. It was almost more difficult than talking to the boys. She chewed on the end of a pencil and reviewed the items on the list. Her head came up when the noise of slamming car doors and muffled voices floated up from the drive at the foot of the stairs that led to her apartment. Alex frowned. She knew from her conversation with Jesse that Mavis and Walter weren't due home until the weekend. Had they cut their trip short so as not to miss the birth of their first grandbaby?

She stepped over to the door and peered through the glass. Her heart sank to her toes at the sight of five women assembling at the base of the stairs, each with a determined look on her face and a casserole dish in her hands. Lucille Humphrey, Charlotte Lawton, Susan Smith, Paula Johnson, and Donna Morrison.

Grace Community's Casserole Crusaders.

Each widowed and elderly and each the embodiment of the idle busybodies Paul must have had in mind when he wrote first Timothy 5:13. A little too helpful, a little too opinionated, enough self-righteous advice to fill a football stadium, and not enough Christian wisdom between them to fill a thimble.

Oh, they meant well, and Alex had been a pastor's wife long enough to know that every church had the same group in some form or fashion. She'd known she'd be forced to deal with them before this thing was settled, but this morning? How was this even possible? She'd been in the apartment less than twenty-four hours. A run down the short list of people who knew her business settled on one name for the leak—Mavis Cooper. Her landlords might still be out of town, and surely Jesse and Walter had cautioned Mavis towards discretion, but the marital spilt between the pastor and his wife had obviously proved too juicy for Mavis to resist. Mavis wasn't a member of the crusaders, but she obviously had contacts in the organization.

Alex stepped away from the door and leaned against the opposite wall, out of sight of the window. There wasn't a back way out of this place, and hiding in the bedroom seemed cowardly. She closed her eyes against tears of frustration. *God, I am not prepared for these women this morning.*

A knock on the door jerked her head upright. The five women were clustered on the tiny landing, faces almost pressed against the glass, each jockeying for the best position.

Ready or not, I guess. Alex pasted a smile on her face, reached for the knob, and pulled the door open. "Ladies."

Charlotte Lawton was first through the door. She shuffled her casserole into one hand and placed her other wrinkled hand over her heart. "Oh, bless your heart, Pastor Alex. Up here all by yourself and crying your eyes out." She patted Alex's cheek as she passed. "Don't you worry. We're here to help get you back on God's track."

Alex's eyes went wide and she stood, speechless, as the others trooped in and put their offerings of food on the bar. *God's track?* Her jaw went tight, aching with a response she didn't dare utter. Freed of their burdens, the women took uninvited seats around the room.

Alex looked from face to face and gave a mental gesture of surrender. The only way to get rid of them was to hear them out. *Polite...be polite.* "Ladies, what an unexpected...

pleasure." She almost cringed at the lie. To make up for it she lifted her nose and sniffed at the aromas wafting from the covered dishes. "Something smells yummy. I just finished a grocery list. I'll need to revise it." She smiled and received five stony stares in return. "Would anyone like coffee?"

Five heads shook in unison as if all five were controlled by the movement of a single puppeteer. The word *Stepford* popped into Alex's mind and, despite her annoyance, she bit her lip to keep from smiling.

Paula Johnson, the eldest of the group, took the lead. "Pastor Alex, if you could have a seat, we'd like to talk with you."

The woman's voice wavered with age or, maybe, pent up emotion.

"Yes, talk." Donna Morrison echoed the words as her hands twisted nervously in her lap. "We're very concerned."

Alex moved into the living area and frowned when she realized the only remaining seat was on the sofa between Susan and Lucille.

Lucille must have seen Alex's slight hesitation because she focused her moist, rheumy eyes on her and patted the spot. "Sit here, hon. We won't bite."

That's a matter of opinion. With no real choice, Alex sat.

Susan reached over and wrapped one of Alex's hands in a blue-veined grip. "We've just come to pray with you."

Alex twisted a bit to meet the older woman's gaze. "Really?"

Paula nodded. "When we heard...well...we didn't believe it at first, but here you are, and Pastor Hunter is nowhere around." Tears welled in her eyes. "My heart aches for this misdirected twist in your path. The Bible is

clear on divorce. There's just no justification for it unless..."
She covered her mouth, her next words squeaking between
her fingers. "Has Pastor Hunter been unfaithful? Have
you?"

Alex lunged to her feet. "What? No!"

"Well, then." Charlotte raised her hands. "Why are you
here? I respect you, Pastor Alex. You've always been an
effective woman of God, but you know God can't use you
unless you are completely obedient."

"And you can't be obedient and not be under your
husband's subjection," Susan intoned.

Alex crossed her arms and pinned each woman with a
stare. "There has been no infidelity in our marriage. We are
not getting a divorce." *No, you already did.* She ignored the
little voice and pushed on. "There are some *private* issues in
our marriage that we are working to resolve."

"Do you feel that the Bible supports your choices?"
Donna asked.

"You know, life isn't about what we want," Paula added.
"It's about what God wants for us."

"You must think about the example you're setting for
the members of Grace Community," Lucille whispered.
"You have young married women who depend on you for
direction."

*Of all the...these women took the cake and all the
sweets at the fair.* Alex turned to face the two women on
the sofa. "And what example would that be, Lucille?" Alex
pushed both hands through her hair and struggled for a
calm she didn't feel. "That pastors are human just like
everyone else? That when two imperfect but forgiven
humans live together long enough, they might come up
against a problem that requires a little time and space to
deal with? Or is it the example of Hunter and me doing

everything Biblically possible to save our marriage that you object to?"

Alex bowed her head and massaged her temples. "Look, ladies. I know you love us. I know you want God's will for us. We do too." She stepped to the door and pulled it open. "Thanks for your show of concern, but I have to ask you to leave. I can't talk to you about our personal problems." She waited silently as the ladies looked at each other, then stood and moved to the door. "I'll see all of you on Sunday."

The Casserole Crusaders filed out with Paula bringing up the rear. The woman reversed course at the door, crossed back to the kitchen, and snatched up her dish. When she passed, she clutched Alex's arm in a vicelike grip. "You should spend some time in the scriptures and learn how a Godly wife is supposed to behave."

Alex shook free and closed the door behind them, impressed with herself that she didn't slam it off its hinges. She leaned against it and looked up at the ceiling. "Father, I love each one of those women, but I don't like them very much right now." Despite her agitation laughter bubbled at the memory of Paula retrieving her dish. The laughter morphed into tears before the last car pulled from the curb.

HUNTER CRADLED a cup of rapidly cooling coffee as he paced the length of Grace Community's auditorium. He hadn't bothered with the lights. He knew every inch of the space as well as he knew his own bedroom. A bedroom he'd spent a very long, lonely, and restless night in.

While he paced, he prayed. Not prayers for his congregation, not prayers for the direction of his next sermon, not prayers for the sick or broken. This morning, he searched his heart and brought himself and his marriage to the heavenly Father he served so faithfully.

Too faithfully?

Was that possible?

Hunter hadn't thought so. He'd considered Alex's periodic demands frivolous right up until he'd found himself hesitating at the idea of spending two nights a week with his wife. The look of disbelief on Dave's face over that one thing had driven doubt deep into Hunter's mind. Doubt that had haunted him all night and brought him here so early. The lyrics of an old song flickered through his mind, and Hunter grimaced as he whispered them aloud. "It's me, oh, Lord, standing in the need of prayer." Even softly uttered, the words echoed in the empty space.

His feet as heavy as his heart, Hunter took the two steps up to the platform, sat in one of the dark leather chairs, rested his elbows on his thighs, and stared at the pulpit while he twisted the cup in his hands. So many years, so many sermons. The congregation of Grace Community had doubled under his leadership over the last ten years. Had he gotten it wrong? Had he missed the will of God?

You didn't miss My will, son. You did outrun Me a time or two.

Hunter closed his eyes, familiar and comfortable with the voice that whispered in his heart. "Father, I've worked so hard to build something special for You, something special for the community. I never did it for recognition or financial gain. I wanted to show people the way to You."

You've done well.

He absorbed the words. "Well? Is it *well* that my sacrifice is about to cost me my family?" The question hung in the silent auditorium. Hunter put his cup on the side table and resumed his pacing. "I'm not oblivious, Father. I've counseled enough workaholic spouses to see the parallels between me and them. But"—he waved a hand around the room in frustration—"for You."

You sacrificed what I never asked you for. Yes, you've worked for Me. That is not the same as working with Me.

The gentle rebuke stung. For...with. Was there a difference? Hunter laced his fingers behind his head and stared at the floor, waiting for God to continue.

Son, there is so much more for you than what happens inside these walls. Just as I sent Jethro to set Moses on a better path, I've sent Dave to speak to you. Change will not be easy, but heed his advice and remember that I work all things for your good.

"What does that mean? Heed his advice about delegating? Heed his words about cutting back? Heed his words about this unnecessary separation? Am I supposed to turn my life inside out?"

Heed his advice.

This time the words carried a finality in the tone that told Hunter he'd heard all he was hearing from God for the time being. Feeling less than enlightened, Hunter retrieved his cup and made his way to his office. If God was done with him for the day, he had work to do, a sermon to finish for Sunday, Bishop Maxwell's project to play with, visits to make, changes to think about.

But, for the first time in a long time, he didn't have a clue where to start. Truth be told, he missed his wife. The bare bones of that reality puzzled him. He rarely saw or spoke to Alex through the day, but he'd counted on the fact that, regardless of what his day held, she'd be home when he got there. Her gentle presence in the room never failed to lift the weight of his day from his shoulders. The knowledge that tonight, and a lot of nights that followed, she wouldn't be waiting weighed his heart down.

He swiveled in his chair and booted up his computer. Mornings were for administrative things, he reminded himself. He'd check his email and see if anything urgent awaited his attention. The first message to pop up stilled his fingers on the keyboard. It was from Alex. He clicked it open.

Morning. I wanted to give you a heads up. I just had a very interesting visit from the Casserole Crusaders.

Hunter's lips twitched. He hated when Alex called them that, but he supposed they'd earned the title. Then her words hit home. A visit? He closed his eyes. Bad news traveled fast in a small town.

They brought food, curiosity, and advice. They weren't here long since I pretty much tossed them out. Anyway, they were concerned about our separation and actually had the nerve to imply that one of us has been unfaithful.

Hunter ran his hands down his face. Of course they did. And if they thought that, others would as well.

Of course they don't know about the divorce...no one will hear about that from me, but it did make me think. As necessary as this time apart is, it was never my intention to put you in a position to defend your morals. I have every intention of attending service at Grace Community during our separation. If nothing else, this time can be a positive example to our church family as they see us working through our problems in a civilized and Biblical manner.

If you have any ideas about how to diffuse the gossipmongers, I'm willing to listen.

Alex

Hunter read the message three times. How could impersonal words on a screen...and the bad news they carried...make him miss her more than he already did? He straightened and typed a response.

I disagree about the necessity of the separation.

He looked at the words and the blinking cursor that waited for his next thought. He backspaced over them. Why start an argument? The separation was a fact.

Thanks for letting me know about their visit. I appreciate your willingness to work with me in subjugating any misguided conclusions our friends might be tempted to jump to. Maybe we should just be honest with them. Let them know, from the pulpit, that no marriage vows have been broken. That we've separated for a set amount of time to work through some problems.

He corrected a word here and there and studied his response. It seemed a bit cold. He added a final line.

Alex, I want you to know that I am willing to work with you on this. I miss you.

Hunter tapped his fingers on his desk. Should he suggest lunch? He really did want to see her. Would that be a violation of their *agreement?*

With a frustrated growl he hit send and stared at the screen, impatient for a response. When the chime sounded, he rushed to open the message.

I think that's a good idea.

His shoulders slumped. Talk about cold and impersonal.

The chime sounded a second time.

I miss you too.

Hunter smiled before he turned away from the screen. There was hope. He bent over his desk and got to work on the message he and Alex would share with their congregation on Sunday.

EIGHT

The rest of Alex's Thursday passed with shopping and cooking. To her pleasant surprise, she'd found the apartment's little kitchen well stocked with pots, pans, bakeware, and a nice supply of kitchen gadgets. Leftovers from Jesse's occupancy or things donated by her friends? She'd ask them in the morning at Soeurs.

By five p.m. the whole apartment was awash in the fragrances of garlic, basil, tomatoes, and oregano. Alex sprinkled salt over a large pot of boiling water and added the lasagna noodles, stirring them carefully as they softened so as not to break them. After a quick stir of her mom's secret sauce, she grated a block of mozzarella cheese and combined it with the ricotta and the parmesan. She spooned a bit of the cheese mixture onto a cracker and dribbled it with some of the sauce, smiling when the combination of flavors hit her taste buds. *Perfect.* If her dearly departed mother knew she stirred all the cheeses together instead of layering them individually, she'd have a stroke, but Alex had learned a few shortcuts over the years. And, since her lasagna was a favorite of the boys, Hunter, and everyone who'd ever eaten a potluck meal at Grace Community, she must be doing something right.

She slid the heavy pan into the oven and set the timer. Setting the timer meant looking at the clock, and her stomach did a sick roll. The twins would be here soon, and, as much as she loved them, this wasn't a discussion she looked forward to.

Father, please help me help them understand that I'm trying to save our family not break it apart. Give me words that accomplish that without being overly negative about Hunter. I don't want either of my babies to feel as if they have to take sides.

The prayer barely left her heart before Alex heard footsteps on the stairs. She had time for a single fortifying breath before the door opened and admitted her sons.

"Hey, guys. You're early."

Benjamin crossed the space and pulled his mom into a hug. "Blame it on the temptation of Grandma's lasagna." He bussed her cheek with a kiss and whispered, "Sean's in a mood."

Alex didn't have time for a response before he released her. She turned to Sean and held her arms open. He stepped into her embrace, but she detected a hesitancy in his manner she'd never experienced before.

He stepped free and offered her a tight smile. "Early was my idea." He broke eye contact and cleared his throat. "We have a lot to talk about. I didn't see the point in dragging it out."

Benjamin looked up at the ceiling. "Bro, you are such a moron."

Sean put his hands on his hips and stared from brother to mother. "I have questions, OK? Get over it."

"Boys." Alex studied her younger-by-four-minutes son,

a little surprised by his jump-right-in attitude. Benjamin was the natural leader of the two, extroverted and outspoken where Sean tended to be more introverted and bookish. She'd planned to have their talk over dinner, where food and drink would occupy their hands and soften a hard discussion with comfort food.

That had been the plan, but their early arrival dictated a change. Alex motioned to the living area. "Have a seat."

The boys settled at either end of the sofa, and Alex took one of the wing chairs on the other side of the room so that she could look at them both. Her gaze rested on Sean. "What do you want to know?"

"What you think you're doing would be a good place to start."

Alex sat back as if he'd slapped her.

"Sean..." Benjamin lowered his head into his hands.

For all that her boys had been raised on the front seat of the church, they were as much boys...young men now...as any males on the planet. Rowdy, opinionated, risk-takers. But in all their years, neither had used such a disrespectful tone of voice with her. She pinched the bridge of her nose, sent up a quick prayer, and leaned forward in her seat.

"Sean, I know that this is a difficult time for our family. It's hard to understand what's driving my actions—"

"Not from where I sit," Benjamin said. "We've shared your struggle. If you lacked for Dad's time and attention, so did we."

Benjamin might have meant his words to soothe, but they ripped deeper. Alex'd done everything she could do over the years to cover up Hunter's neglect and misplaced priorities. It stung, a lot, to know she'd failed.

"That's horse hockey, Ben," Sean growled.

The boys looked at each other, mouths tight, nostrils

flared. In that moment, Alex could see the very different men they were becoming despite the fact that outwardly, they were carbon copies of each other.

"Dad had responsibilities—"

"He had a family," Benjamin said. "One he shouldn't have had if he didn't plan to help raise them."

"Well," Sean sneered. "We all know now how unintentional that was."

Benjamin lunged to his feet and leaned over his brother. "You take that back."

Sean came out of his seat and stood toe to toe with Benjamin. "Make me."

"Boys!" Alex angled between them, put a hand on each chest, and literally forced them apart. "What's gotten into you two?" She faced Benjamin. "Your father loves you even if he doesn't always express it in the way he behaves." Her focus went to Sean. "You two were the biggest surprise God ever allowed me to have. You have been loved and wanted by your father and me since the second we knew you existed."

She stood between them until she was sure some of the anger had dissipated. "Now, there are things between your father and me that are our business. I won't be discussing any of that with either of you. As far as what I was thinking when I moved out..." Alex stepped away and faced her boys with crossed arms. "I am hoping to create a *controlled* situation where we can remember why we fell in love in the first place. God willing, when this is all said and done, we'll be a stronger family for it."

The oven timer dinged. "Your dinner is ready. Let's sit down and enjoy it. While we do that, I'll be happy to answer any questions you might have about how this process is expected to work."

"Sounds like a plan," Benjamin said.

"You two enjoy." Sean crossed the short distance to the front door. "I'm out of here."

"Sean, don't—" The door slammed on Alex's plea, and her eyes swam with tears as she looked from it to Benjamin and back.

Benjamin took a quick step and gathered her into his arms. "It's OK...he'll be OK. He's just conflicted right now."

Alex shrank against him as tires shrieked in the driveway.

"Can I tell you a secret?" Benjamin asked.

Alex nodded against his chest.

"OK, but you need to act surprised when Sean tells you."

Alex stepped back and looked into Benjamin's eyes. Eyes that looked so much like Hunter's that she had to swallow before she could answer. "OK."

"He feels like he's called to the ministry. He planned to tell you guys at dinner the other night, but...well, we got distracted."

Alex looked back at the door. "Oh, no."

"This whole thing between you and Dad has him confused about his direction. But you know Sean. He just needs some time to process. That and he's working up the courage to share this with his girl. He and Ashley have talked about the future, but not a future in the ministry. This whole thing is sort of bad timing."

"My poor baby."

Benjamin put an arm around his mother's shoulders and squeezed. "Mom, I know you worry about us, but do you think God has a plan in all of this?"

"I know He does."

"Then let God work it out, for you and Dad, and Sean."

He turned her toward the kitchen. "While God's working, I'm starving. Feed me."

Alex grabbed pot holders and slid the bubbling lasagna out of the oven. "Get the salad out of the fridge, will you? I just need to turn up the heat and put the garlic toast under the broiler for a couple of minutes." She looked at the huge dish. She'd be eating lasagna for a week. "Will you take some of the leftovers home for Sean? I made German chocolate brownies for dessert. They're his favorite."

"Well..." Benjamin sent his mother an impish grin. "Yes to the lasagna, but the brownies...I don't know that he deserves them."

Alex narrowed her eyes.

"But, yes."

"Thanks. Oh..." Alex glanced back at the door. "Since Sean left, do I need to drive you home?"

Benjamin shook his head. "We drove our own cars. I'm going to go hang out with Kinsley for a bit after dinner." His expression bordered on devilish. "You know how you women get when your men don't pay you enough attention."

The words stung until she saw the twinkle in his eyes. The towel Alex threw at his face missed him by a hair.

"DAD."

Hunter looked up from the desk in his office and the open Bible in front of him. "Sean." He marked his place and slid the book to the side. "Come in. This is an unexpected surprise." He motioned to a chair. "Sit. What brings you home, and to the church, in the middle of a school week?"

"Really?" Sean stepped into the room but didn't sit. Instead, he circled the room like a nervous animal. He trailed his fingers along the spines of books on a shelf, straightened a picture, and plucked a peppermint from a bowl. He studied the candy, hesitated, and dropped it back in place.

Hunter folded his hands on the desk and waited. Of his two sons, Sean was the thinker, where Benjamin was the doer. When Sean had something on his mind, he needed time to examine it from every angle before speaking. Pressing him would only stall the conversation.

The boy mumbled something, and Hunter straightened. "What?"

Sean turned and spread his hands to take in the space. "I've always loved your office. I'd hoped to have one just like it someday."

Hunter cocked his head. "Like..." Pride leapt. "Like this? You mean a minister's office?"

Sean nodded and turned away. He picked up a book and flipped through the pages, speaking with his back to Hunter. "I've felt a...tug...something...in my heart for a while now. A desire to serve I can't seem to get away from, even though I've tried." He put the book back into place and turned to face his father, his hands lifted in surrender. "Benjamin has his future in business administration all mapped out. Locked, loaded, unwavering, but me? I've done two years at OU, switched my major twice, but nothing seems to fit."

Hunter studied his son. He'd hoped one of his sons would follow him into the ministry. But, honestly, he'd hung those hopes on Benjamin, the more outgoing of the two. Sean seemed uncomfortable just thinking about the ministry as a career path. "Until now?"

He nodded. "Until now. Pretty lousy timing, don't you think?"

"Son, I'm not sure I'm following you."

They stared at each other in silence for a few moments before Hunter continued, "I get it that you feel like God is calling you to the ministry. I'm extremely proud that you're willing to listen and give that calling due consideration. I don't understand why you feel the timing is off."

"You and Mom—"

"That situation has nothing to do with you or your decision to go into the ministry."

Sean stared at him. "How can you say that? You and Mom are splits. That by itself makes it a bad time for me to think about transferring."

Transferring? Had Alex forgotten to tell him something? Or had she told him and he'd not been listening? No. He'd definitely remember that. "Where are you—?"

"Oregon."

Hunter sat back. That would not sit well with his mother. Which meant she didn't know yet. At least he wasn't that far behind.

"I've got some online friends who highly recommend it." He waved the question of the transfer away. "It doesn't matter. I can't leave with things so unsettled at home. And what about you? If Mom stays gone, your time here, your ministry, is pretty much over." Sean sat and bowed his head. "You and Mom doing ministry together here at Grace Community...that's been my rock. Something I always knew I could depend on. An example of what two dedicated people could accomplish for God. Yes, we all made sacrifices, but they were for a greater purpose, weren't they? Underneath it all, I thought we had a solid family. Now? I don't have a prayer of convincing Ashley that ministry is the life for us if my own parents throw in the towel." He ran both hands through his hair. "I don't know what to do."

Hunter looked at his son, speechless. He'd never heard Sean say so much in a single conversation. When had he and Ashley become so serious? He'd bet money that Alex could give him date, time, and place. He closed his eyes at this newest reminder of his lack of attention where his family was concerned. *Father, give me some wisdom here.*

"Sean, it's been brought to my attention in a forceful fashion that I have a lot to learn about a great many things, but let's take your concerns one at a time. First of all, if the ministry is what you're called to, then nothing else you try is going to make you happy. Have you prayed about it?"

Sean straightened. "Yes, sir. Do you remember that camping trip I took back in the fall?"

Hunter nodded. "You and several friends from school went up to Robber's Cave."

Sean squirmed in his seat. "I might have exaggerated a bit there. It was just me and Levi Tillis, a youth pastor friend of mine. We did camp, but we spent the long weekend fasting and praying about our futures. That's when I sort of got my answer."

"Then you should pursue it. Oregon...well, we can talk about that. If that's where you want to go to school, you're an adult, and Mom and I will support your choice. As for what's happening between Mom and me, it's temporary. I'm sure your mother has assured you that she is doing everything she can to save our marriage. Let me add my voice to that. The fact that we aren't living together doesn't mean we've given up. There is work to be done, but neither of us is willing to give it less than our all."

Hunter closed his eyes and prepared to admit a bitter truth. "You said we all made sacrifices, and you'd be right.

But it seems that some of those things were...less necessary than others. I'm going to be working through some issues in the upcoming days, but I already know that I owe you, your brother, and your mom an apology. Where you and Ashley are concerned, I'll say this. Your mom and I like her very much, and you'll have our blessing if you decide on a future together. Doing ministry as a couple can be the most rewarding thing you'll ever do. Even what your mom and I are facing right now doesn't change that truth. Just don't make the mistakes I have. Guard every second of your time. Pray about every decision, and look for God's direction every day."

He stopped as the advice he'd just given his son speared Hunter through the heart. How many times had he rushed blindly into an opportunity, a program, a project without prayer, without thought, without considering the time it would take away from his family?

Hunter bowed his head and offered up a silent prayer. *I'm sorry, Father. Please give me the wisdom I need to exercise that advice in my own life.*

NINE

Alex's feet were heavy on the stairs leading to the workout room at Soeurs Friday morning. She was exhausted after a night peppered with nerve-rattling vignettes starring the Casserole Crusaders and a very angry Sean. Most of the details of her nightmares had gone fuzzy, but one stood out in stark relief in her sleep-deprived subconscious. Paula Johnson knocking at her door with a huge pot of something rancid smelling. When Alex let her in, she set the pot on the counter and whipped off the lid. Inside Sean was swimming around in a vile stew. When he saw her staring down at him, he began shouting at her. She'd jerked awake before any of his words registered, or maybe God in His mercy hadn't allowed her to remember what she was sure were hurtful words. She reached the landing and leaned her head against the door frame. *Father, I'm so tired, and it's only day two of a four-week process. I know You have a plan even if I can't see it. Would You care to share some details?*

She allowed a dozen heartbeats to pass while she waited for an answer. When nothing came, she pulled in a deep breath and pasted on a smile. The women behind the door respected her privacy, but if she went into that room looking like she felt, all bets were off. Her smile slipped. Not being able to share this heartache with her friends was one of the hardest things she'd ever faced. She didn't want or need their sympathy, but she longed for...Alex searched for a word and came up empty.

"You know what it is, Father," she whispered. "When Mac was so lost, when Randy was so sure she'd lost Eli for good, when Charley had to face Melissa after all those years, when Tyson wouldn't leave Jesse alone, when Syd had to face the scars Donny left behind, we were a unit, sharing those burdens. I need that right now. Thank you for Lisa, but I feel so alone."

Daughter, you are never alone. Listen, they are lifting you up to Me even as you despair.

Sounds faded from the stairwell. The soft whisper of the air conditioner, chatter from the technicians working on the ground floor, even the early morning noise from the street outside subsided as Alex's hearing narrowed to the muted sounds on the other side of the door.

Muffled words floated through the door. "Father...Alex and Hunter...love...heal...they need...the boys...help us... them." God didn't let her hear everything, but what she heard flooded Alex's heart with peace and straightened her shoulders. She was acting like a spoiled ninny. Even without knowing the details, her friends were doing what they could do, and she would do what she could do. In this moment, that meant facing those precious women with a smile. Alex grasped the doorknob, gave it a rattle to warn them she was coming in, and pushed open the door. "Morning all."

"Hey," Randy said. "We weren't sure if you'd make it in this morning."

"Oh?"

"We sort of heard you had a bad night," Syd said.

"Really?" Alex looked at each of her friends in turn, stopping when she came to a guilty-looking Charley.

Charley cleared her throat. "Benjamin came to see Kinsley last night. He was pretty upset. He didn't tell us anything," she reassured quickly, "just asked us to pray for everyone and called his brother a moron."

Jesse crossed her arms and cocked a hip. "I prayed for Benjamin not to be such a bully. I know what a pain in the backside big brothers can be."

A real smile twitched at the corners of Alex's mouth. "Thanks, ladies. All prayers appreciated. Despite common myth, twins don't always coexist in harmony." Her gaze slid to Mac, seated on a folding chair like a queen holding court. "Speaking of...how are Aria and Adam doing today?"

Mac's fingers circled the T-shirt covered mound of belly. "Danielle and Allen are fine."

Alex stared at her very pregnant friend, hands on her hips. "Danielle and Allen? How many names have you guys discarded since Wednesday to get to that?"

Mac bowed her head. "A lot."

Her shoulders shook, and Alex rushed to her side. "Oh, sweetheart, don't cry, I didn't mean—"

"I'm not crying, I'm laughing," Mac gasped as she raised her head and wiped at the moisture on her cheeks. "I was over in the store next door before I went home Wednesday. Dane introduced me to Ember... Ember Pelletier...the craft lady."

"I've met her," Jesse said. "She needed a CPA to help

set up some of her business stuff and Dane sent her to see me. I really like her."

"Me, too," Mac said. "Anyway she mentioned a friend with twins named Aiden and Serena. I liked those names but Dane didn't. Set us off on the hunt again where we came up with Danielle and Allen. Today, I'm calling them that, but I'm not quite sure they sound right." She bit her lip. "It's ridiculous! I'm ready to give up. At this point I'm perfectly happy to call them Baby One and Baby Two until they start school. Then they can tell Dane and me what they want to be called, and everyone will be happy."

Charley knelt next to Mac. "You're making this harder than it needs to be."

"You think?" Mac narrowed her eyes. "I'm a crazy woman. I actually considered Buffy and Jodie."

"I like those names," Jesse said.

"Really? You want your niece and nephew named after a pair of orphaned twins from a sixties sitcom?"

"Oh..." Jesse drew the word out. "Obviously before my time."

Alex patted Mac's hand. "I know you're feeling pressured to make a decision, but maybe you should put it out of your mind for now. The second you look into those precious little faces, the fog will clear, and you'll just know who they are." She smiled up at the nervous mother-to-be. "Honestly, it's probably going to be the very first names you thought about."

Mac leaned back in the chair and twisted to her right and then to her left. "I don't even remember what those were."

"You will." Alex straightened. "Now, I think it's my turn to lead our workout." She bowed to Mac. "At your pleasure, Mommy, just tell me where to start."

"Start with some jumping jacks." Mac grinned when Alex winced. "Don't be a baby. A quick set of twenty-five to get the blood pumping. Next some simple stretches, and then, once the music starts, you can make it up as you go along. I'll let you know if I see you slacking. Fifteen minutes of floor exercises, then circuit, then stretches."

"You're the boss." Alex took a spot at the front of the room. "Randy, some music please. Let's get our praise and our fitness on."

As Alex's body settled into the familiar rhythm of the moves, she breathed a sigh of relief that went up as a prayer. *Thanks, Father. My friends, my routine, and Mac's mommy woes were just what I needed today.* Jumping jacks complete, she crouched into a series of lunges. As the other women scurried to match her movements and Mac watched each of them with a critical eye, Alex put her heart into the workout. She'd soothed her soul with comfort food last night —two glasses of ice cold milk and three of the rich brownies —and she had excess calories to burn.

When she and Hunter said "I do" for the second time, and Alex clung to the hope that God would work that out, even if she wasn't sure what it would look like once He did, she wouldn't face her husband with an additional five pounds of chocolate stacked around her waist.

Oh, Father, please work this out. I love Hunter, but I can't fix him. That's up to You.

"Hold up."

The sound of Mac's voice startled Alex out of her thoughts.

Mac waved at Randy. "Pause the music for me." She pushed out of the chair and waddled over to Syd. "You're going to hurt yourself like that. Crouch into the stretch. Let's see if we can improve your stance." When Syd complied, Mac used her own foot to nudge Syd's back a half step. "Bend your knee a bit more." She looked at the repositioned Syd. "That feels more natural, doesn't it?"

While Mac worked on Syd's execution, the others took a few good-natured potshots at Syd for causing the interruption.

"It's bad when the preggo has to show you how it's done," Jesse muttered.

Randy wiped sweat from her forehead. "Yeah. How long have we been doing this routine?"

"Y'all hush," Syd gave Mac her full attention.

Charley ignored them all, left her place on the mat, and took a few swings at the punching bag.

Alex jogged in place to keep her heart rate up and let the normality of it all wash over her like a warm ocean wave. Normal had been just what she needed this morning.

———

ACROSS TOWN, Hunter's routine was anything but normal. He sat behind his desk and watched the door close behind the fifth person in the last forty-five minutes. Five people, five requests that didn't amount to half a hill of beans, and five thinly-veiled mining expeditions for information he wasn't about to share. He rubbed at his temples and drew in a deep breath. He needed to get some work done before his visitation time. It was Friday, and he'd promised Bishop Maxwell an outline for the men's retreat by next week, and he didn't have a single thought on paper as yet.

He raised his head and stared at the closed door, mentally daring anyone else to knock. When several seconds passed in silence, he booted up his computer, opened a new Word document, and typed in a title.

Building Godly Families in an Ungodly World.

Hunter's fingers froze on the keyboard, and he sat back and read the title. Seven simple words that seemed to mock him. How could he begin to teach on a subject in which he'd failed so miserably? Maybe a better title for his series of sermons would be, *How to lose your family while saving everyone else's.* Or...even better... *How to neglect your family in six easy steps...* How about the oldie but goodie...*Do as I say, not as I do.*

He dropped his head into his hands as that final pseudo title filled his mind and shamed his heart. The answer to his question was that he couldn't. If he tried he might as well have a big H for hypocrite tattooed on his forehead.

Hunter clenched and unclenched his hands a few times before bringing his fingers to the keyboard. If he backed out now Bishop Maxwell would have plenty of time to get someone else to fill the job. He typed, thanking the Bishop for the opportunity and citing a family emergency that had arisen since their conversation a few days ago. He listed the names of three or four other ministers for consideration and hit send before he lost his courage. Stepping away from this obligation wasn't the easy thing, but under the circumstances, it was the right thing.

Before he could close out of his email the incoming chime sounded.

Pastor Conklin, good morning. Allow me to introduce myself. My name is Levi Tillis, I'm a friend of Sean's.

Hunter frowned at the screen. Levi Tillis...the name was familiar, but... The light bulb of recollection flickered to life. Oh yes, the young man Sean had gone camping with a few months ago. The memory of last night's conversation with Sean brought a smile to Hunter's face. His son had depths Hunter had yet to explore. Sean's friendship with Levi was part of the reason his son was investigating his own options for the ministry. He returned to the email.

I know that this note is going to take you by surprise. Believe me when I say that I've never done anything like this in my life and wouldn't recommend this sort of out-of-the-blue contact for anyone looking for a job, but God's being pretty insistent that I write to you this morning and, proper avenue or not, I've found that God never works on just one side of a problem. If He's bugging me so insistently, He must be speaking to you as well, so here goes.

I've been the youth pastor at Stonebrook Fellowship for the last four years. I've enjoyed the position and I love the kids, but I feel like God is nudging me out of my comfort zone and into the next step of my ministry training. I've talked to my current pastor and boss, Isaac Cox, about this move, and he is in full support of my decision, so please feel free to contact him as you see fit.

I know that this is going to sound more than a little presumptuous, but I am writing to offer my services to you and Grace Community as an assistant pastor. I've attached my resume for your convenience. I understand that this is not the way things are normally done, but I've lain awake for three nights trying to talk God out of this lunacy. He won't let it or me go. I hope you'll take a look at the resume and then join me in prayer about working together in the future.

Yours in Christ,

Levi Tillis

Hunter studied the note. His knee-jerk reaction was to send it straight to the delete folder, but his hand was frozen on the mouse and refused to obey his command to move the cursor to the trash button. He read the note a second time and, instead of seeing a brash young man, too self-important for his own good, he got hints of just how much courage it had taken to step out in such obedience. He raised his eyes from the screen and looked at the ceiling. *Father, You're going to have to let go of my hand so I can open the attachment.* With that prayerful thought, his hand came loose, and the mouse skittered across the desk. Hunter brought the mechanical little rodent back to his mouse pad and clicked on the attachment.

He studied Levi's qualifications and a glowing letter of recommendation from Pastor Cox. The boy looked more than qualified to move into the position he was applying for. Trouble was, there was no position available. Dave might think it was a good idea, but Hunter didn't see how he could take the time to train a new staff member right now. He was already in more trouble than he could handle with Alex over his schedule. Adding something else to it wouldn't work. He pressed his lips into a firm line, typed a quick line of acknowledgment to Levi. He'd pray about it as the young man requested, and if God changed his mind, he could contact Levi through Sean. He sent the whole thing to the trash.

The note disappeared from his inbox just as a knock sounded at his door.

Hunter put his head in his hands, squeezed the bridge of his nose, and kissed the hope of a productive morning good-bye. "Come in."

When the door swung open, Hunter looked up to see six men standing in the doorway. His heart did a little sideways skitter as he motioned Grace Community's entire church board into his office and watched as they found seats around the room. The space was more than adequate for seven people, but Hunter suddenly found it hard to draw a breath. The expressions on the men's faces were too serious for this to be a casual chat, especially when most of them had jobs. Jobs they'd obviously taken time from in order to be here.

While they settled, he laced his fingers on his desk and sent up a quick prayer for wisdom and direction. He was a preacher, not a rocket scientist, but he didn't need a degree in jet propulsion to know why they were here. This group was several steps above Alex's Casserole Crusaders, but the coming discussion wouldn't be any less tedious. He decided not to allow them the opportunity to dissemble.

"Gentlemen, can I get anyone anything to drink before we get started?"

Jack Hightower, the senior member of Grace Community's board, leaned forward in his chair and allowed his clasped hands to dangle between his knees. He looked at the floor for a few seconds before raising his head to look Hunter in the eye. "Pastor, you know that you can count every man in this room as your friend, and we want to keep it that way, but...well...we thought we ought to come to you in an official capacity. We're concerned...about you and Pastor Alex and Grace Community."

Hunter nodded. "Thank you, Jack. I appreciate your candor, and Alex and I appreciate your concern. I know that the situation between my wife and me has put the board in an unusual position." He motioned to his computer. "I wrote a letter of explanation to the church yesterday. Alex and I intend to present it to the congregation on Sunday. I'll be happy to print off some copies and allow you to read it in advance. I probably should have called each of you and offered that already, but things have been..." Hunter searched for a good word and failed to find one. "Well. Just let me get those copies."

"Thank you, Pastor, we'd like that," Jack said. The others nodded in agreement.

Hunter turned back to his computer, found the document, and sent a request to his printer for seven copies. The silence in the room, broken only by the laser printer's shuffling noises, weighed on him. When had he ever sat with any of these men in silence for more than a few seconds at a time, much less minutes?

Finally, the printer spit out the last sheet. He kept one and handed the rest to Jack, who distributed them around the room. More silence as the men read. One by one, they finished and looked up.

Jack took the lead once again. "This helps, Pastor."

Leon Jasper cleared his throat and raised his copy. "We were hoping...praying...well, we..." His face turned a bright red.

"What Leon is trying to say," Daniel Morris said, "is that we're relieved there's been no infidelity. None of us wanted to believe it, but...the world is a messed up place."

Charles Boulton flicked the corner of the papers. "You'll swear that there's no reason for concern there?"

Hunter swallowed back a sudden flash of anger. These men had been elected to keep the trust of Grace Community. He wouldn't berate them for doing their job. "Yes, Charles. My word of honor." Something dark and heavy left the room.

Afton Gilbert lifted a finger for attention. "Pastor, we're very relieved to see that this separation is being moderated by a Christian counselor and grateful that it has a limited time frame. You anticipate reconciliation in a month?"

"That's the plan."

Harry Harper edged into the conversation. "What can we do?" He made a motion that encompassed all of his brethren. "We've talked about it. We'd be happy to send you guys to one of those fancy marriage retreats, at the church's expense, if you think that might help."

"You and Alex have been a blessing to our church for a lot of years," Charles said, "but if things don't get resolved in a reasonable amount of time, we...well...it's a decision we'd hate to make, but we can't keep you on as pastors if divorce enters the picture."

Hunter sat back in his seat and studied Charles. The ominous words carried more worry than threat. A worry that Hunter had been trying to ignore since Wednesday.

"Good grief, Charles. What's wrong with you?" Leon sputtered. "You don't bring threats into a situation like this."

Hunter raised his hands. "I didn't consider it a threat. The most important thing anyone can do for us is to respect our privacy during this time. I promise I'm not going to neglect any of my ministerial duties while we work this out, but I'm going to need some time to—"

"And that's another thing," Jack said. "We've talked about this too. The time thing that is. There's no way to gauge its effect on your family, but even a blind man could see that our congregation has outgrown one man's ability. Maybe it's time to think about bringing in a second pastor—"

"Only as an assistant," Afton reassured.

"God's blessed us. We can afford a second salary," Harry offered.

"Yes," Jack continued. "An assistant, someone to help with the day to day." He looked at Hunter. "What do you think of the idea? Will you pray about it?"

Hunter blinked and glanced at his computer and up to where he imagined God hovering over the room, directing this meeting. Dave, his board, Levi Tillis...a perfect stranger.

How was it that everyone but he himself, the man in the foxhole shoveling for all he was worth, saw the problem and the solution so clearly? Maybe he needed to take a step back and let some of the dust settle.

"Yes." The word whispered out of his dry throat. He swallowed before trying again. "Yes, brothers. I think that's a prayer-worthy idea. Thank you for being so generous."

TEN

Sunday morning, Alex took her normal place at the piano as service at Grace Community got started. She sent a quick nod toward the wood-and-glass drum cage. The young drummer acknowledged her signal, beat his sticks together a couple of times to set the tempo for the first song, and the church swelled with worship music.

She fingered the keys by rote. There was nothing new on the program this morning, and she could play the *regulars* in her sleep. She let her gaze wander the unusually packed sanctuary. *Of course packed. Everyone wanted to see the next act of the Hunter and Alex show.*

Normally, when she played, she lost herself in the music, oblivious to the people in the pews and what happened around her while she offered her talent for music back to God. Today was different. Today, she felt like one of two fish in a bowl. She and Hunter were more than pastors this morning, they were oddities. Guilt poked at her. She'd put them in this position. If she'd just acquiesced to Hunter's plan, they'd be remarried by now, and none of this would be happening. She straightened. Hope for a better future with her husband wouldn't be happening either. They'd have run across the state line and come home to the status quo. Instead, she held onto a little optimism for the future. Alex needed that more than she needed breath.

Her gaze roamed the sea of faces. She saw a good mix of anticipation and confusion as friends and the people they'd pastored for years wondered what happened next. But, sprinkled here and there, she saw hurt. Alex ached over the hurt, ached over the knowledge that she was partly to blame.

In self-defense, her eyes sought out the faces of her friends. Mac and Dane sat five rows back on the right closest to her. He rubbed her shoulders, and she petted the huge mound of belly in time with the music. Almost as if she felt Alex's eyes on her, Mac looked up and sent her friend a smile.

Randy and Eli sat across the aisle and three rows further back. Randy's green eyes lit when Alex looked her way. She'd obviously been waiting for the connection. *You've got this*, the redhead mouthed.

Syd and Mason were sitting next to Jesse and Garrett, smiles in place. Jesse shoved her glasses up and sent Alex a nod of support.

Alex searched for Charley and Jason and found them standing against the back wall. They were both in uniform, which meant they were both on duty. Alex hoped they had time to stay to hear the explanation she and Hunter were about to offer. This morning would release her from part of her duty-bound silence. No one must ever know of the divorce, but after she and Hunter finished this morning, she'd feel like she could be a little more forthcoming with her friends on some of the minor issues.

The worship team lowered their microphones and took

a step back. Alex's hands dropped into her lap while the final notes from piano, guitars, and drums echoed and faded into the rafters. That was Hunter's signal to take his place behind the pulpit. Normally, he'd rush on stage like a kid given free rein in a toy store. He'd start with some announcements and prayer requests, then take the morning offering while enthusiasm for the sermon he was about to deliver sparked around him like static electricity.

But this morning when he stood, Alex couldn't help but notice that his steps dragged instead of bounced. His shoulders were a little slumped, and a grim smile replaced the welcoming one that normally greeted his congregation. When he reached his place, he didn't look out over the gathering. Instead, he stared down to where his Bible and notes rested.

Alex saw his shoulders lift, and she heard his bracing breath from twenty feet away before he turned to her and held out his hand. Her stomach churned, and an invisible weight settled onto her chest. *Now?* Didn't he have something to do, something to say to ease them into this moment of conflict? She swallowed against a sudden bout of nerves and saw his gaze pleading with her to join him. In a daze, she scooted back from the piano and crossed the platform to Hunter's side. He didn't say a word as he took her hand and leaned over to place a quick kiss on her cheek. The touch of his lips broke the trance of fear. Oh, she still loved this man. She didn't have to be told that he felt the same. Beyond the years of misunderstanding and neglect, love bubbled. In this time and place, putting their marriage and what ailed it first was the right thing to do. It was the only thing to do if they wanted to continue their work here at Grace Community with the people they loved.

HUNTER SQUEEZED her fingers but didn't release her hand. He straightened and looked out over the morning's worshipers.

"If you guys would stand with me for a second, I'd like to begin with prayer."

Papers crinkled, fabric rustled, and the wooden pews creaked as hundreds of people scrambled to their feet.

When they were standing, Hunter closed his eyes. "Father, thank You. We've already felt Your presence among us this morning, and we're grateful. Let Your continued strength and wisdom be manifest in our service today. We ask for Your divine direction from this moment forward so that all things might be done in a manner pleasing to You. We ask these things in Jesus' name."

He finished the prayer and, when the gathering had settled back into their seats, an unnatural silence descended over the sanctuary. As a minister, he always worked to capture this group's undivided attention. This was not the way he'd wanted to get his wish. Hunter released Alex's hand and unfolded a printed copy of what he'd given the members of his board on Friday. He didn't need the notes, as the contents were burned into his memory, but the action gave him a few additional seconds for his heart to stop pounding and his hands to stop shaking. He adjusted the microphone attached to the pulpit and spoke.

"As most of you know by now, Alex and I have separated." He paused, taking in a gasp here and there. Apparently, there were a few people not connected to the grapevine. "We wanted to take some time this morning to assure you that, even as we work toward a resolution to our personal problems, we will both continue to be available to you and the ministry here at Grace Community. We also wanted to assure you that there has been no marital infidelity on either side." He paused and swept the room with a stern glare. "Rumors to the contrary or speculation in this area are both unjustified and unwelcome." He let that sink in for a few seconds before going back to his notes. "But, there are some serious issues that need our attention, issues that we felt..." *Alex...Alex felt.* But he didn't say it, just cleared his throat and continued, "We felt warranted some extra space while we sought God's will and direction. During this time, Alex and I will be working with a Christian counselor under established guidelines and a set time frame to bring our marriage back into the context ordained by God in the second chapter of Genesis." He paused to look at Alex. Tears streamed down her face, but there was a smile as well. The smile bolstered him.

Hunter turned back to the congregation and leaned forward. "Alex and I have counseled many of you through marital difficulties over the years. We've done our best to support you while respecting your privacy. We ask that you extend the same grace to us, and we are grateful in advance for your prayerful support and understanding."

He folded the paper and tucked it into his Bible before taking Alex's hand a second time. He rested their clasped hands on the edge of the pulpit in full view of the congregation. "I want to finish this by saying that God blessed me with an amazing wife when I was too young and too stupid to appreciate such a gift. Sometimes, I don't think I've gotten much smarter over the years. With God's help and her patience, I'm going to do what I can to fix that."

He looked at Alex. There were tears on her cheeks, but she was looking at him as if he were the three-legged calf at the county fair. Part astonishment and part disbelief. Had his words—that mini admission of guilt and a promise to fix it—shocked her so much? Maybe *stupid* was too mild a word for what he'd been.

ALEX SWALLOWED HARD. Had he...had her husband just admitted to...had he just made a public promise to fix things? She felt suddenly light. *It's going to be all right.* Alex closed her eyes and let all of her conscious thought narrow to the feel of her hand in his. Continued frustration over the situation poked at her, but that hand holding hers reminded her of just how much she needed his strength and the warmth of his steady presence beside her. Not just this morning, in this moment of scrutiny, but every single day. She exhaled, and her gaze went to the ceiling. *Father, we've made a mess. Please show us how to fix this.*

"Alex, did you have anything you wanted to say?" Hunter asked.

She jerked back to the moment. Did she want to add anything to the prepared statement? Not really, but she would. She loved these people as much as Hunter did. It was important that they know that. She took a half step toward the microphone, maintaining her grip on Hunter's hand as if she were about to cross over a patch of quicksand and the ground might swallow her up. With the other hand, she dabbed at her streaming eyes and nose with a crumpled tissue.

"I just want you all to know how much you are loved. From the bottom of my heart, and Hunter's. I know this situation is hard to understand. I think pastors and their families are expected to be above this sort of problem. But, we're people first, just like each of you." Her eyes zeroed in on the pew where the Casserole Crusaders sat in a disapproving clump. Her focus narrowed onto Paula Johnson for a second. "I told someone the other day that it's my hope that Grace Community will be strengthened by the example of their pastors doing everything they can to find a Biblically correct solution to our problems. I—"

A loud gasp to her right drew her attention as Mac surged to her feet.

"Mac?" Alex asked.

Mac looked at the floor and put a hand on Dane's shoulder. Even at a distance, Alex could see her friend's face stained red with embarrassment. "Um...I think my water just broke."

"I'm gonna be a daddy!" Dane scrambled to his feet, swooped his wife and the forty extra pounds of baby weight into his arms, and carried her out of the building. Randy, Syd, Jesse, and Charley left their places and followed them out of the auditorium. Alex watched them go. Looking from the door to Hunter and back again.

"Go," Hunter stepped back from the mic and spoke to her under his breath. "I'm pretty sure that was the end of service this morning. No way I can preach a message that tops this. I'll be there as quickly as I can."

"Have everyone pray before you dismiss." Alex's throat clogged at the memory of her own difficult delivery and those first uncertain days. "She's not due for another month or so."

Hunter squeezed her hand, obviously reading her thoughts. "Go," he repeated. "God's got this, just like he had us."

Alex nodded, stepped from the platform, and snagged her purse from her customary seat on the front pew. She rushed down the center aisle, already digging for her keys. *Father, please...*

By the time Alex reached the hospital, the staff had Mac admitted, and she and Dane were cloistered away in one of the labor-and-delivery rooms. "Any word?" She dropped her bag into a chair and pushed moisture damp-ened hair from her face. Somewhere along the way, a spring shower had kicked up. Despite it being Sunday morning, she'd been forced to park in the nether regions of the visitor lot—with no umbrella.

"She's fine," Randy said.

"Grinning ear to ear once the embarrassment of disrupting service wore off," Jesse offered.

"Down to the wire and still worrying about names," Charley answered.

Alex dismissed all that with a wave. "Good to know, but she's early, and she hasn't had a baby in twenty years. What did the doctor say?"

Syd, the only one of the four who'd actually had a baby, grinned. "Haven't seen the doctor, but the nurse assured us that mother and babies are doing fine. Strong fetal heartbeats and an attentive father-to-be standing by to address Mac's every need." She shook her head. "The poor guy has no idea what he's in for. I called Anthony horrible names and almost put his hand in a cast before Sara came. Childbirth is not for the fainthearted."

Alex remembered her similar experience with a smile. "Yes, but we forget the pain, and daddy will forget the abuse. When can we see her?"

Jesse glanced at the clock. "Shouldn't be long. They said we could wander in and out once they got her settled, but no more than three visitors in the room at a time." She crossed her arms. "That's practically my whole family in there. I get dibs on one of those spots for the day. I want to be there when Jackson and Jacqueline make their appearance."

Alex cringed at the names. "Seriously?"

Charley ran a hand through her shaggy blond hair. "That's what Mac said when they wheeled her away."

"I think we need to have a prayer meeting for God to erase those names from her memory," Randy said.

"We're going to love them regardless of their names." Alex changed the subject. "Did someone call Riley?" Mac's son would want to be here, of course. "Jesse, what about your parents?"

"Mac said she called Riley from the car," Jesse answered. "He's on his way. I called Mom and Dad. They were already on their way home, but they spent the night in Albuquerque. That motor home drives like a tank, so they're at least eight hours out." Jesse paused and rubbed her ear. "Mom screamed so loud when I told her the babies were on the way, I think my eardrum is permanently damaged."

Alex looked around the room, and the absence of all the husbands registered. "What did you do with the guys?"

Syd smirked. "Mason said this was no place for men and suggested that they go to lunch. We allowed it on the condition that they bring us food when they come back."

"We included burgers and shakes for Hunter and Riley in that order," Charley said.

Alex nodded. "Fast food, the twenty-first century equivalent to boiling water and clean towels."

Randy's green eyes twinkled. "Exactly."

"Excuse me."

The women looked up to find a frowning nurse in the doorway. The older woman wore starched green scrubs—

plain green, not the cheerful prints Alex had seen the other staff wearing. She stood ramrod straight, disapproval rolled off her in waves. "Mrs. Cooper is in Room Four. She has requested that all of you be allowed to step in for a moment. Please make it a brief moment. We've established our rules for the comfort and safety of mother and baby. Too many people in the room make for too much excitement in an already stressful situation."

Whoa... Alex looked from the nurse to her friends. Five heads nodded in agreement.

"Come with me." The nurse, her steps brisk but silent on the tile floor, led the way.

"Stuffy much?" Jesse said. "Who does—?"

Alex did her best to smother a giggle as Charley sent an elbow into Jesse's ribs to shut her up. They entered the room right behind the nurse and found Mac in bed, her eyes closed, her knuckles white and tight around Dane's hand. Alex glanced at the monitor and saw the graph coming down on the end of what looked to be a healthy contraction.

The nurse rushed forward and patted Mac's hand. "There," she said. "That was a good one. Those little ones are eager to meet you." She wiped Mac's brow with a cool cloth and handed her a cup of ice. "Your friends are here."

Mac grinned her gratitude. "Thanks, Estelle. We'll make it quick."

Estelle nodded and left the room.

"Isn't she the best?" Mac asked. "It's like she can read my mind. This is so much different than the tiny country hospital where I had Riley. Technology has changed so much, it's sort of intimidating, but Estelle seems to know my questions before I can even ask."

Alex pressed her lips together and saw Randy do the same. Jesse regarded her sister-in-law with her hands on her hips. Syd and Charley found something interesting outside the window.

"Yep, well...Estelle said you wanted all of us?" Alex asked.

Mac nodded. "Just for a quick prayer. I'm trying not to worry, but they are coming early. I want Analise and Aiden to be healthy."

Alex swallowed laughter. "Well, God is already on the move in this situation."

Mac's eyes went wide. "Dane..."

When Mac's eyes fluttered closed, Alex touched the mound of baby and felt the muscles of Mac's abdomen grow rock hard beneath her hand. "I think I agree with Estelle. These are very impatient babies. Ladies." She motioned the women into a circle around the bed, and everyone joined hands.

"Father, Thank You for Mac and Dane," Alex said. "They're about to start the most important job of their lives together, and these two precious babies are blessed to have them. Be with Mac. Give her strength and peace. Give Dane calm and patience. Watch over this little family, Father. Keep everyone safe in your hands today. In Jesus' name we ask these things."

A throat cleared from the doorway. Estelle was back. She sent a pointed glance at the clock.

Alex looked at Dane. "You need anything?"

"A splint." He shook his hand and sent Mac a smile brimming with love. "No, I'm good."

Alex leaned down and whispered in Mac's ear. "Try not to kill him. God's got this. We'll be right outside."

ELEVEN

At lunchtime on Monday, Alex shooed Dane and Riley out of Mac's hospital room. It was hard to tell which was the most in love with the sleeping babies, the proud papa or the awed big brother. Jesse, Garrett, and Dane's mom and dad were waiting in the lobby to take everyone out to lunch. Even though Mac was asleep, Alex decided to sit in the quiet room while they were gone. A few minutes surrounded by the lovely smell of baby wash and new baby sounded like the perfect way to spend an hour. Aimee and Zachary slept as peacefully as kittens full of fresh milk. She'd never wake one of them on purpose, but if those precious babies stirred, maybe she could keep them from disturbing her very tired friend.

She bent over the first plastic bassinet and studied the baby swaddled in a blue blanket. A little card in a built-in holder read Zachary Dane Cooper, seventeen inches long, five pounds, three ounces. Alex traced a light finger around a tiny ear while her heart ached with tenderness. "Welcome to the world, little guy."

A soft mewl drew her to the second bassinet. The baby's

arm waved free, and Alex gently tucked it back under the pink blanket. Rosebud lips made a sucking motion for a few seconds before the baby stilled. This card read Aimee Beth Cooper, seventeen inches long, four pounds, fifteen ounces. When she glanced from the card to the baby, Alex found unfocused blue eyes staring in her direction. It was all the excuse she needed. She gave her hands a quick wash at the sink and scooped up the tiny bundle. It felt like she was holding air. After snagging one of the hospital-sized bottles of formula, just in case, she and the baby settled into the recliner next to the window for a get-acquainted visit.

Alex held the tiny baby girl close to her chest, closed her eyes, and rocked. There just wasn't anything better in the whole world than a freshly minted, perfectly formed, gift-from-above baby. "We're going to be friends, you and me," she whispered. "You can call me Aunt Alex, and I'm going to be your mommy's go-to babysitter." Aimee wrinkled her nose, and her little mouth formed an O before she smiled. It might have been a gas bubble, it might have been a tiny fart. Alex chose to take it as a show of agreement and antic-ipation.

"We're going to have monthly shopping trips full of pink lace and fancy, girly lunches. Don't worry. If you prefer denim and fast food, we'll compromise." The baby worked a hand free of the blanket a second time. Alex took it and studied the tiny, dimpled fingers. "You have amazing fingers, girlfriend. Would you like to learn to play the piano? I can teach you. I always wanted to teach my boys, but if it didn't include a dirty ball of some shape or fashion, they weren't interested."

Aimee's face stretched in a huge, toothless yawn, and her little eyes drifted closed. "That's OK. You and your brother had a big night. We'll talk when you've had some rest." Alex snuggled the baby closer, put up the footrest, and felt her own eyes grow heavy. That was another thing about babies. She'd never been able to hold a sleeping infant without being lulled into sleep herself.

A noise jerked her out of the almost nap. Hunter stood at the door, an uncertain look on his face. How long had he been standing there? Alex glanced at the clock over the door and realized it was time for his daily hospital rounds. She motioned to the cluttered sofa under the wide window. He wasn't getting the baby, but she wouldn't chase him away.

"You sure?" Hunter whispered.

Alex nodded, silent while he made his way into the room.

Hunter moved Dane's blankets and pillow to the side and sat on the edge of the cushion as close to Alex as he could get. He leaned forward, hands between his knees, to study the baby. "She's beautiful."

Alex didn't respond, just bent her head to place a light kiss on the mass of dark curly hair.

"Where is everyone?"

"Lunch," Alex murmured. "I'm babysitting. Aimee and Zachary arrived just after one this morning. Mac is exhausted. Dane is still walking on air. They might have to tether him to his chair like one of those big Macy's Thanksgiving Day parade floats."

Hunter's eyes sparkled at the image. Even holding the baby, Alex had a second of longing. How long had it been since he'd looked at her with anything but impatience? *Umm, like...yesterday.* She conceded the point to her conscience. Yesterday had sparked some hope in her heart, but it was going to take more than a pretty speech to his congregation to show her he meant business.

A soft noise from the other baby drew her attention.

"Hurry," she hissed. "Wash your hands and grab him before he wails and wakes Mac."

Hunter scrambled to do as he was told. Alex watched as he leaned over and scooped up the baby. He was a pro. No warning to support Zachary's head was needed. He settled the baby in the crook of his arm and came back to the sofa. He sat, held the baby tight against his chest, and buried his nose in the thick black hair. Alex swallowed a chuckle. She'd never met anyone immune to the smell of new. New cars, new puppies, new babies. Some things were universal and genderless. *New* was one of those things. When Hunter sat back, there was a look of wistfulness on his face that took Alex by surprise.

"What?" Alex asked.

"It's just..." He looked up and one shoulder lifted in a shrug. "Never mind."

Alex narrowed her eyes.

He shook his head. "It's just us, sitting here, both holding a newborn. It brings back a lot of memories...good memories."

Alex looked down into Aimee's sleeping face. "We were so young...so clueless." She chuckled against the baby's downy head. "Sometimes I look back and wonder how Sean and Benjamin survived."

"You raised two amazing boys."

Alex looked up at his use of the singular pronoun.

"You heard me. You raised our sons to be responsible, moral adults. My contribution was secondary. I intend to make up for that if they'll...you'll let me."

She studied him. The sincerity she saw in his expression tugged at her love for him and begged her to give him the chance he was looking for. *Chance two thousand.* Her heart's reminder boosted her resolve to see the separation out. "We're working on it."

The baby in his arms squirmed for attention. Alex handed Hunter the bottle, and he teased the little lips with it until they latched tight and began to suck. "What if I told you that I've already seen the light. That—"

Alex's snort of disbelief cut across his words. "Twenty-plus years of marriage"—she kept her voice a low whisper—"countless discussions about what your family needed and deserved, and you want me to believe that, after less than a week of separation, you've come to see my point of view? Please."

Hunter didn't respond for a few seconds as he took the bottle out of Zachary's mouth, raised the baby to his shoulder, and patted. Once the baby burped, he lowered him and replaced the nipple into the hungry little mouth. "Hard to believe, I know. But it doesn't always take a lightning bolt to get my attention. Just call me Moses."

Alex frowned at him, her retort unusually sarcastic. "That's a little lofty, don't you think?"

"You can thank Dave Sisko for the comparison. He likened my single-minded focus to Moses's experience in the wilderness. Once I took a long look at the story of how he was killing himself trying to be all things to all people, it didn't take me long to draw a few conclusions."

Aimee started her own hungry protests, and Alex rose to get a second bottle. "Do tell."

"I began to wonder how Mrs. Moses must have felt, watching her husband march from their tent every day, knowing that by the time she saw him again, all his time and energy would be spent. Problems with the boys would fall to her, issues with their household...her again. Unfair is not an adequate word. But the harshest part was that, at the end of this little mental newsreel, when Mrs. Moses looked at me...I saw your face."

Alex concentrated on Aimee. If she looked at Hunter right now, she'd weep. This wasn't the time or the place, but she wanted her husband to keep talking. She'd waited years for this. Out of Hunter's vision, Mac stirred in the bed. *Not now, Mac. Go back to sleep.* In answer to her silent command, Mac gave a small sigh and snuggled deeper under the covers.

Hunter continued, "The next part of the story is where you need to pay close attention. Once Moses had God's direction, he didn't argue about it, didn't put off the changes, he just made them. I'd like to think that the first thing he did was apologize to his wife for being misled."

Again his choice of words captured Alex's attention. "You think God misled—?"

"No, I think I misled myself by not seeking direction." He stood and laid the sleeping baby back in his bed before coming to stand next to the chair where Alex sat. "I've messed up and I'm sorry." He bent down and dropped a kiss on Alex's head. "Meet me for dinner tomorrow night. Not here in town. Let's try that new steakhouse out on the highway."

Alex just looked at him.

"I know we aren't supposed to discuss our problems on our *dates,* but I've got some things in the works that will help you see how serious I am about fixing what I screwed up."

His admission of guilt knocked the props out from under Alex and forced her into a brutal honesty. "We," Alex whispered as she looked into the face she loved beyond her own life. "In the good or the bad, it's always been we."

"And it will be again. Meet me tomorrow night, six-thirty?"

Unable to speak, Alex nodded.

HUNTER STEPPED off the elevator into the lobby. His step was light and there was a smile on his face. Not the I'm-a-pastor-I need-to-be-approachable smile he wore when he was in public, but a genuine smile of happiness. He was taking steps to fix his troubled marriage, and the whole thing was oddly empowering. *I'll cut this separation nonsense in half.*

His feet froze. Was that all his change of heart was about? Ending the separation? He sank into one of the seats in the hospital's lobby and examined his motives. Something inside had shifted over the last few days and, upon further inspection, Hunter found his initial frustration with Alex's defection taking a back seat to a real desire for change. So, yes, he wanted his wife back, but not for the same reasons he might have listed a week ago. He wanted her back because he loved her. He wanted to find a way to show that love to her every day for the rest of both their lives. How could he do that?

He drew his hands down the length of his face. He knew Alex would be happy having him home for dinner two or three nights a week. But the change happening in his heart was so complete that he didn't just want to settle for making her happy. He wanted her swept off her feet, excited to spend the rest of their lives together.

The divorce remained their first obstacle. They needed to get remarried in a way that tied up the legalities, assured

Alex of his unending love, and left no one the wiser about their youthful mistake.

His memory went back to the boys and their desire to do something special for their parents' anniversary. Maybe he could do something special and involve the boys. Planning something for Alex would be a great project to show his sons that Hunter was serious about making up for some of the time he'd wasted. It wasn't just Alex he owed an apology to.

He could work a lunchtime visit to Norman into his schedule this week. Visit with the boys and engage their help in planning that trip Alex wanted so badly. He grinned. Not just a trip, a cruise. His wife loved the ocean.

Another weight fell off Hunter's shoulders. He'd always loved his wife and family, even if he'd not been the best at showing it. The way he was feeling, he almost expected to see the green skin and red eyes of a Christmas cartoon character the next time he looked in a mirror. He searched his memory for a name and came up empty. But he remembered the guy's heart growing three sizes in a single moment of revelation. The way his heart pounded indicated something was under drastic renovation. He inched one eye open and looked down at his hand, found it the same color as always, and uttered a quick prayer of thanks.

Galvanized, Hunter looked at his watch. He still had several hospital visits to make, but he needed to go back to his office first. He wanted to look up some information on cruises and call the boys. First, he needed to retrieve that resume and catch up to Levi Tillis. That assistant pastor thing was looking better and better every second. The sooner he could set up a meeting with that young man, the better.

TWELVE

Alex snuggled into the corner of her couch with a cup of coffee Tuesday morning. Living alone had a few perks she hadn't anticipated. The opportunity to fix an early morning breakfast and invite her friends without the worry of disturbing someone else in the house was oddly refreshing. And unlike the Casserole Crusader gathering of a few days ago, she relished her company this morning.

Randy, Charley, Jesse, and Syd, all dressed for their day, each with a steaming cup of coffee and a plate piled with pancakes and bacon, lounged around her tiny living room since there was no dining room in the small apartment. Alex had no desire to live like this forever, but, while she did, she'd take advantage of the unique opportunities her situation offered. Unique opportunities...like a date with her husband. She'd been married to Hunter for almost twenty-three years, but the thought of their date tonight made her breath catch in her throat. The last few years had drained their relationship of a lot of things. Intimacy had been a victim, right along with trust. Alex missed the primal comfort of his body next to hers. Her face heated in a blush.

She bowed her head and allowed her chestnut pixie cut to curtain her face. Now was not the time to think about... She swallowed and forced her mind back to safer topics.

Moses.

Yep, old men with long beards. That was the ticket.

Hunter's whole thing about Moses had intrigued her. Alex was more than curious about what Hunter had to say tonight. She was hopeful that things would change for the better sooner rather than later.

How long has that hope been springing?

The little internal voice was snide and sarcastic, and Alex smothered it under a breath of prayer. *Jesus, I'm counting on You.*

"These are amazing."

Charley's words brought Alex back to the present.

"Secret recipe?" Charley asked around a bite of the fluffy stack on her plate.

Syd speared her own bite, held up her fork, and motioned to Randy. "I don't know about you, but I might be late for work. I'm having seconds, and it'll be an hour before I can move."

Randy nodded her agreement. "That's fine. After this we won't need lunch. We can lock ourselves in my office, prop up our feet, and take a nap."

Syd held her fork out, and Randy clicked hers against it. "Innovative ideas like that are why you're the boss," Syd said.

"I'm telling Mac on both of you." Jesse cut a dainty bite, swirled it through the syrup on her plate, and popped it into her mouth. "When she gets back to work, I can sit back and watch her make you sweat."

"Snitch."

"Tattletale."

Syd and Randy spoke over each other before cutting another bite.

"Speaking of Mac. How's our new mommy doing?" Charley asked. "I looked in on her after work last night, but she was sleeping."

"Yeah, she slept most of the day," Jesse said. "She was worn out after twelve hours of labor. Dane and I took care of the babies as much as we could, and Mom and Dad were in and out. I think they're sending everyone home in the morning." Her expression turned dreamy. "Aimee and Zachary are so stinking cute. I want one."

The room went quiet.

"Really...?" Randy drew the word out. "Something you'd like to share."

"No!" Jesse declared. "I mean...we're working on..." Her words faded while her cheeks flamed red.

"Newlyweds," Alex laughed. "Hunter and I got some cuddle time yesterday, as well."

Charley leaned forward. "Do tell."

"Baby cuddle time," Alex clarified. "It brought back some nice memories."

As one, the women set their plates aside. "That was really sweet," Syd said. "Sunday, I mean. I know I'm sort of the newbie, here and at church, but I think everyone felt a little better hearing things from both of you."

"We hoped so." Alex took a sip of her coffee. "It took about six hours after I moved out for some ugly rumors to start circulating. We needed to set the record straight for everyone's sake."

"So how does this controlled separation thing work?" Jesse asked.

"Jesse," Charley hissed.

"Oh, hush." Jesse frowned at the cop. "I'm not being

nosy, and I'm not asking for any details Alex can't share."
She looked at Alex. "It's just...well, you guys seemed really
at ease with each other Sunday. You just said you were at
the hospital together yesterday... I'm curious. Most people I
know who are separated go out of their way to avoid each
other."

"Sunday was necessity, yesterday was accidental." Alex
smiled up at the ceiling. "But tonight...that's intentional."

"What's tonight?" Randy asked.

"Date night, our first." Alex leaned forward, eager to
share her excitement. "Like I said. Yesterday was accidental,
but something happened while we held those babies.
Hunter opened up in a way that...well...in a *not Hunter*
way. He's taking me to dinner tonight, and, girls...I'm about
as excited as a homecoming queen on the arm of her favorite
quarterback. I really feel like things are about to turn
around."

The questions pelted her like a driving rain.

"Where are you going?"

"When was the last time you had a pedicure?"

"What time?"

"What are you wearing?"

Alex took them one at a time. "The new steakhouse out
on the highway. My toes are fine. Six-thirty. Slacks and a
blouse, I guess." She flinched under the collective looks of
her friends.

"Oh, no you don't." Jesse jumped to her feet. "Come
with me." She disappeared down the short hallway.

By the time Alex and the others caught up, Jesse was
buried in the closet, rummaging through hangers like a
bargain hunter at a half-price sale. "Slacks and a blouse,"
she muttered, shoving clothes this way and that. "Please..."

She stuck her head out and pinned Alex with a pitying stare. "Did you not pack anything even remotely dressy?"

Alex shrugged. "I—"

"You're going on a date," Jesse continued. "This is beyond your everyday casual wear."

Alex huffed and nudged Jesse out of the way. She reached in and pulled out a black skirt. "Fine, I'll wear this and a blouse."

"Hmm..." Randy looked at the simple linen skirt. "I almost agree with Jesse. Tonight is sort of a big deal for you guys. Do you have something better at the house? If you don't want to go over there, tell us what you want and where it is. One of us can go get it for you."

"I don't see the big deal." Alex looked from one woman to the other, finally settling on Charley. The cop...the sensible, pragmatic one.

Her uniformed friend shook her head. "Repeat after me...date."

"With my husband."

Syd put her hands on her hips. "You need to make that man drool in his salad."

Alex choked on a snort of laughter. She'd been excited about tonight, but it was just dinner with Hunter. Or was it? Could it be more? "I have that blue dress I got for last year's New Year's Eve party. It's not fancy, but I've only worn it once."

"It's perfect," Jesse said.

"That dress looked great on you." Syd's eyes widened. "I just got a new blue, black, and silver duster. It's exactly what you need to turn that dress from classic to atomic."

"Duster?" Alex frowned.

"That's what I call it. One of those shear, drapie,

hangie-downie things." Syd made motions around her legs. "It sort of swirls around your knees when you walk. Sexy."

Were these ladies determined to kill her? "You girls." But fresh anticipation sparked like a flame in dry tinder. *Maybe just a little sexy.* "Shoes... If I'm shooting for sexy, I need new shoes." She looked at her toes and then her hands. Maybe she'd get that mani/pedi while she was out.

HUNTER ZIPPED through the routine of his day on Tuesday, moving from one task to the next with the skill of a master juggler. When a water pipe in the men's restroom sprang a leak, Hunter called Dane. Not for a repair, but to ask the new father if he had someone to recommend for the work.

The new guy ran late. Waiting on him deprived Hunter of breakfast and delayed the start to his visitation schedule. In all of this, he still hadn't been able to get through to Levi Tillis, but he had his cell phone number. If God was really behind the timing of all this—and how could He not be?—the boy would catch up with him eventually.

Hunter finished with his hospital rounds and settled into a convenient, fast food restaurant for a late lunch. Halfway through his crab cakes and shrimp his phone rang with a number he didn't recognize. His first thought was *finally.* He swallowed a french fry, chased it with a drink of his soda, and swiped the call open.

Expecting Levi, he was a little taken back when a woman answered his greeting.

"Hunter Conklin, please. This is Eve Morris returning his call."

The travel agent. Well, retired travel agent with great

contacts. At least that's what Eli Page had told him after he'd sworn the man to secrecy. Couldn't have him blabbing to Randy and Randy leaking his intentions to Alex.

"This is Hunter Conklin. Thanks so much for returning my call."

"I'm sorry I missed you yesterday. My husband and I just returned from a small vacation, and we didn't arrive home until late. What can I do for you?"

"I'm interested in getting some info about a cruise. My wife and I will be celebrating our anniversary soon. I'd like to surprise her."

"What a lovely idea. Have you guys ever cruised?"

"This will be our first."

"When did you want to leave?"

"Sometime in the next three to four weeks," Hunter answered. The pause on the line didn't fill Hunter with a lot of hope. "Problem?"

"Well, that depends on a lot of variables. Length and destination mostly. For first-time cruisers, I generally recommend four to five days. That way, if either of you proves to be a poor sailor, you aren't stuck out in the middle of the ocean for too long. Where did you want to go?"

Hunter laughed into the phone. "Eve... May I call you Eve?"

"Of course."

"Eve, if I had the answers to all of those questions, I wouldn't have called you. You've got a complete novice here. Tell me what you'd recommend."

Eve tsked into the phone. "So many choices. There are numerous four- and five-day cruises to the Caribbean. The most accessible of these leave from Galveston, Houston, or Louisiana ports. You can cruise to the Caribbean or the Bahamas from Florida as well. Do you have passports?"

"My wife does. She went on a mission trip with the youth group last year. I've never had a need."

"Hmm...That could be your biggest issue right there."

"I thought you could cruise without a passport."

"You certainly can, but I never recommend it. If the unforeseen happened and you needed to return home in an emergency, you'd be stuck. You can cruise into the Caribbean with no passport, but you can't fly out of there without one."

Hunter mulled this info. He was turning over a new leaf, and he wouldn't be on-call for this trip, but he didn't like being without options.

"I'll get one."

"I don't think you understand," Eve told him. "Passports can take as long as six weeks to process, sometimes longer, even if you pay to have it expedited. I can book you on a cruise without it, but this close to sail date, there's no guarantee you'd have it in time. We can insure the fare, you wouldn't be out the money—"

"But I'd have a disappointed wife," Hunter finished. Not a risk he wanted to take. He'd disappointed her enough. "Is there someplace we can go without passports?"

"There are numerous Alaskan and Hawaiian options, but those generally fill up quickly, and none of them are less than seven days. Add travel time on either end, and you're gone for nine days or so."

The old Hunter would have balked. The new Hunter thought nine days alone with his wife sounded like an amazing adventure. "Let's do that. What's available?"

"I'll need to do some research. Can I call you back this evening or tomorrow?"

"That's perfect. I look forward to it."

Hunter disconnected the call and slid his phone into his pocket. It rang a second time before he could release it.

"Hello?"

"Pastor, its Missy Lytol." A woman's voice sobbed into the phone.

"Missy, what's wrong?"

"It's Eric. The police just called. There's been an accident. A car ran a stop sign and crashed his motorcycle."

"Is he hurt badly?"

"I don't know. I'm on my way to the hospital in Henryetta. Can you come?"

"Of course." Hunter looked at his watch and calculated the time it would take to make the nearly seventy-mile drive. "I'm on my way." He dumped his half-eaten lunch and headed for his car. His phone rang a third time.

"Hello."

"Pastor Conklin, Levi Tillis here."

"Levi, yes. I wanted to speak with you about the email you sent, but something's come up, and I'm afraid it's going to have to wait a day or two." He unlocked the car door and slid behind the wheel. "What's your schedule like?"

"I'm leaving on a mission trip with my youth group first thing in the morning. We'll be gone for ten days."

Ten days? Hunter grimaced. "Is there any way you'd be free later today? It might be much later depending on what I find." He told the boy about the frantic call he'd just received. "I can call you when I'm headed back this way. I'll meet you someplace between Garfield and Norman. We'll have a late dinner while we talk."

"That's perfect. I'll wait to hear from you."

Hunter swiped the call closed, and programmed his GPS for the Henryetta hospital. It was going to be a long night.

THIRTEEN

Alex did a quick spin in front of the mirror. The blue dress, draped in the shimmering duster, was anything but simple. Her new strappy spring heels added two inches of height. The pedicure had been the perfect pick-me-up, and the polish she'd picked for her toes made her feel like a new woman all the way to her bones. She jerked to a stop, and her outfit fluttered to rest around legs made firm and shapely by years of thrice weekly workouts with Attila the Hun at the helm. *Thank you, Mac.*

Alex glanced at the time. Almost six. She grabbed her bag and paused for a final look. She smiled at her reflection when she remembered Syd's words. Drool in his salad was the least of Hunter's worries for this evening.

Alex sat in the car outside the steakhouse and watched for Hunter. The parking lot was filling up, and, middle of the week or not, they were going to have to wait for a table if she didn't grab one soon.

She waited behind two families at the hostess desk, breathing a sigh of relief when they were taken directly to tables. The hostess looked at Alex.

"Dining alone?"

"No, there will be two of us. If you could seat me and then bring my husband back when he gets here."

"Of course. Your husband's name?"

"Hunter Conklin."

She made a note, gathered two menus, and handed them to a young man dressed all in black. "Just follow Justin. He'll get you settled and be your server tonight."

Justin led Alex to a table for two in a dimly lit corner. He held her chair as she sat, shook out her napkin, and draped it over her lap. "May I get you something to drink?"

"Two iced teas, sweet."

"Of course." He hustled away.

Alex took a look around the restaurant. It wasn't large, but it was homey, maybe two steps above casual and one below *fancy*. No loud music blared through the speakers nor did TV screens flicker in every corner. The wait staff all wore black, and there were white tablecloths on every table. If the smells coming from the kitchen were any indication, they were in for a delicious meal.

Justin came back with two glasses of tea, a couple of small plates, and a basket of steaming yeast rolls wrapped in a black napkin. He arranged everything in front of Alex. "Did you want to order?"

"Not yet, but keep an eye out. My husband should be here any second."

He nodded and went about his business.

Alex sipped her tea, buttered a roll, wondering what Hunter wanted to talk about. Had God really shown him a different path in just a few short days? It was possible. God was a master at directing His children, especially when they took the time to ask. She nibbled the crusty roll—they really were yummy—and watched the door. Several times she sat up straight, certain that Hunter was on his way in, only to sink back on a breath when it wasn't him.

Justin stopped by the table. "Is there anything else I can get for you while you wait?"

Alex gave him a smile. "No, I'm good. Could you point out the ladies' room?"

Justin did so, and Alex retreated to check her hair and her makeup. She studied her reflection. She really did look good tonight. Alex didn't feel like that was vanity. More than anything she wanted Hunter to look at her the way he used to. She wanted to see the spark of longing in his eyes that had been absent for way too long. She looked at the dainty silver watch on her wrist. Almost seven. He was probably waiting on her now, and she was dawdling in the restroom. Her grin was impish. Good. She could make an entrance. Watch his expression as she approached. The thought did funny things to her insides.

HUNTER DROVE BACK into Garfield at six-thirty Tuesday evening almost five hours after being summoned to Henryetta. Eric Lytol had a few scratches and bruises, five stitches in his chin, and they were waiting on X-rays to confirm a broken wrist.

Hunter shook his head. He wasn't a doctor, but a wrist bent like Eric's was broken, no X-ray needed. Anyway, once they confirmed that the wrist was broken, the ER doc would splint it and send Eric and the films home to see a local doctor for further treatment.

God was good, and Eric and Missy were blessed. They'd shown Hunter pictures of the motorcycle, and he was amazed that Eric wasn't dead.

Eric had thanked Hunter for his presence and his prayers and urged Hunter to go home. Regardless of the results, they wouldn't keep him overnight in Henryetta, and there was no reason for Hunter to linger.

Worn out from the drive and the hectic day, Hunter went straight to his office, checked his messages, and dialed Levi Tillis.

Levi was quick to answer. "Hello, Pastor. Everything OK with your injured member?"

"He has a broken wrist and a few stitches. Other than that, nothing a few days rest won't cure."

"Praise God."

"Every single day," Hunter agreed. "We don't deserve His mercies. You free?"

"At your service."

"Good, I'm starved. You like Mexican?"

"I do, and I'll save you the trouble of driving to Norman. That little place in Garfield...Mama Rosita's. It's on my favorites list. I can meet you there in thirty minutes or so."

"That's perfect, Levi. I'm looking forward to our chat. See you then."

Once the call was disconnected, Hunter took a few minutes to print off a copy of Levi's resume. It was pretty impressive, but there were a few things he wanted to ask about. He already knew the younger man couldn't start for almost two weeks. Hunter didn't like the idea of a delay, but he couldn't ask the young minister to leave his youth group hanging the day before a trip. Hunter read the entire document again and made a few notes in the margins. He stopped when his stomach growled and looked at the time display on his computer. Almost seven. He gathered his papers, turned off his light, and went to his dinner meeting with Levi Tillis.

ALEX RETURNED to the table and found it empty. Her shoulders slumped. *Where is he?* Justin met her with raised eyebrows. "You know what?" she told him. "Why don't you go ahead and bring our salads? I'm sure he won't be much longer."

"Yes, ma'am."

Alex settled in her chair. Had she missed something? She pulled her phone out of her bag and checked for messages. *Nothing.* She weighed the device in her hand. Maybe she should call him. An all too familiar ache started at her newly polished toes and worked its way up to her heart. *Not happening.* He'd made this date. He'd claimed some amazing change of heart. No way was she going to call him and remind him of where he should be.

When the salads came, Alex dug into hers like a starving woman. She had no appetite, but she'd be hanged before she allowed him to show up and see her waiting like...like...well, she just wouldn't. Each swallow diminished the veggies in the bowl and the hope in her heart. When the bowl was empty, she pushed it aside and looked at her watch. Seven-thirty.

I'll give him fifteen more minutes.

Something roiled inside of her and erupted into the voice of reason.

Fifteen more minutes for what? So I can sit here and look more pathetic by the second?

Alex closed her eyes and accepted the truth. He wasn't coming. She caught Justin's eye and asked for the check. She didn't miss the pity in his expression, but she refused to acknowledge it.

She paid the bill and hurried back to her car.

I won't cry. I won't cry.

Each protest lent speed to her steps even as her feet threatened to sink into the asphalt.

I won't cry.

I should have known better. A sob escaped. She could read her husband like a large print book filled with single syllable words. The title of Hunter's story would never change. It would always be *It is What it Is.*

Alex got the door open and the seatbelt buckled before the scalding tears blinded her.

HUNTER THANKED the waiter for the basket of chips and the small bowls of salsa and queso. He salted the chips, spooned some of the restaurant's homemade salsa into the warm cheese dip, and scooped it into his mouth. He was a few minutes early, but he was starving. His schedule had been disrupted from the get-go today. No breakfast, an interrupted lunch, a long drive...

Ah...that's good. He scooped up a second bite, his stomach growling in gratitude. He hoped Levi got here soon. The chips were amazing, but he wanted something more substantial. Hunter looked up when the door opened a few minutes later. The young man that entered was tall and lanky with a head full of dark hair. He wore slightly faded jeans over scuffed athletic shoes. His shirt was wrinkled from the day with the sleeves rolled up to his elbows. He turned in Hunter's direction. The bowtie around the boy's neck screamed geek. Hunter swiped his mouth with the napkin to cover a smile and scooted out of the booth, hand extended.

"Levi?"

The younger man gripped the offered hand in a firm shake. "Pastor Conklin, good to meet you."

The men took their seats in the booth and faced each other from opposite sides of the table.

"You haven't waited long, have you?" Levi asked.

Hunter waved at the half empty basket of chips. "Just long enough to get a head start on these."

"Thank you," Levi said to the waiter when the man slid cheese and salsa in front of him. He dipped a chip, shoved it into his mouth, and crunched. "Can't blame you for that."

The men studied their menus for a few minutes for the benefit of the hovering waiter and placed their orders— chicken fajitas for Hunter and beef empanadas for Levi.

"Empanadas?" Hunter asked.

"You've never had them?" When Hunter shook his head, Levi continued, "They're like little meat pies from heaven, and they're next to impossible to find." He picked up another chip and waved it in no particular direction. "There's a chain of Mexican restaurants that serve them, but the closest one is fifty miles away." Levi paused, his eyes searching the room. "See the older guy over there with that huge tray of food? That's the owner's brother. I went to school with his son, Randall. I talked Randall into going to lunch with me at the chain place a couple of years ago"—he lowered his voice—"sort of a reconnaissance mission into enemy territory, you know? Once he tasted the empanadas, I had to order a second plate because he scarfed all of mine. He took one home to his aunt." Levi sat back as the waiter returned and placed a plate of crispy half-moon shaped pastries in front of him.

"Jesus, thank You for this food," Levi said before he slathered one of the little meat pies with cheese sauce and guacamole. He forked up a healthy bite, chewed, and swallowed with a rapt expression. "And the rest is history. They actually do them better here. Want to try one?"

Hunter watched the younger man through the steam rising from his own plate. His first impression of Levi Tillis was a positive one. Friendly and approachable with just a hint of humor in his telling of the empanada story. "Sure." He cleared a small space on the edge of his plate. "Thanks," he said when Levi placed half a pastry on his plate. Hunter spread a flour tortilla with sour cream and pico de gallo, piled on meat and cheese, and rolled it tight. Once both men had taken the edge off their hunger, Hunter leaned forward. "So, you grew up locally?"

"Graduated from Garfield High," Levi answered. "Three years ahead of Sean and Benjamin. I knew who they were, but we weren't friends then. Now we are...well, I'm friends with Sean anyway."

"You knew he was called to the ministry?"

"Umm..." Levi waffled his hand back and forth over the table. "I knew he was leaning in that direction. Now that he's made up his mind, I'm trying to answer as many questions for him as I can. I told him he needed to talk to you."

"I'm grateful for—" Hunter's phone rang. He frowned at the number. "Sorry, I need to take this." He swiped the call open. "Hello."

"Mr. Conklin, Eve Morris here. I have that cruise information for you."

Everything in the room disappeared at the sound of the travel agent's voice. *Cruise...Alex.* Hunter looked at his watch, groaned, and brought his fist down on the table hard enough to rattle the flatware. *Stupid, stupid, stupid...*

ALEX SAT in her car until the crying jag faded. Her cell phone rang, but she didn't look at it, didn't want to talk to anyone...couldn't talk to anyone. It quit ringing and immediately started again. Alex yanked it free and stared at the screen where Hunter's name and number were displayed.

"Nope." She tossed the phone into the empty passenger seat and started the car. *Not interested.* The phone rang a third time before she could pull out of the parking lot. A vein in her temple pulsed with every ring. She snatched it up.

"Leave me alone." The words scratched out of her throat like a nail file on a broken nail. "I'm not interested in anything you have to say."

"Sweetheart—"

Alex wiped the connection closed. *Who does he think he's kidding?* She threw it onto the floorboard as she pulled into traffic.

There. If it rings now, I can't reach it.

And it continued to ring. By the time she stopped at the single traffic light in Garfield and retrieved the annoying device, she had a dozen missed calls and just as many text messages from her husband. While she waited for the light, she deleted the messages without reading them and then accessed Hunter's number and blocked it.

Alex climbed the stairs to her empty apartment and collapsed in a chair. She'd left two hours ago with such anticipation and returned with her hopes dashed. Hunter's betrayal hurt more than she could have imagined. Shouldn't she be used to it by now? The mixture of rage and bitterness that bubbled in her heart frightened her with its intensity. She reached for the phone in desperation and dialed Lisa.

"Hey, girlfriend," Lisa said. "I didn't expect to hear from you. How was your date?"

Alex swallowed sobs. "It wasn't."

"What?"

"He stood me up."

"Oh, no..."

"I waited for an hour. Like a fool. He finally called about thirty minutes ago."

"What did he have to say?" Lisa asked.

"I don't know. I hung up on him and blocked his number."

"Oh, hon, you need to talk to him."

"Why?" Alex practically shouted the word. "So I can hear him say how sorry he is at another broken promise? I don't care if he's sorry. I've heard "sorry" from that man more times than I heard "Mommy" from the twins in twenty years." She swallowed. "Mommy, Mommy, Mommy, Mommy, Mommy, Mommy, Mommy, Mommy, Mommy, Mommy, Mommy, Mommy, Mommy." Alex's voice broke and forced her to stop. "There," she said on a sob, "and we still aren't even."

"Oh, Alex, I wish I knew what to say. Can you meet Dave and me at the church office in the morning at ten? We'll see if we can figure something out."

"Sure, why not?" Alex disconnected the call and hugged her arms around herself. "God, I thought...I wanted..." She took a deep breath and tried to focus, her prayer whispered aloud. She needed words of truth right now, and she needed to hear them.

"Jesus, I've spoken Your name over this situation. I believe in the power of Your name and the authority that comes with it. There is power in that authority and promise. I believe in the results of Your promises. Your name never goes out in vain, and I trust Your plan for my life even when getting there doesn't look like what I imagined."

Tears stung the back of her eyes like salt in an open wound.

"I don't know what to do. I don't know what to believe."

Trust Me, daughter. I have a plan.

Alex sat up and forced herself into a quiet she didn't fully feel, waiting for some further clue about a plan she couldn't see.

When nothing came she wrapped herself into a tight ball in the oversized chair and cried.

FOURTEEN

Lisa looked up from the coffeemaker when she heard the heavy glass door to the fellowship hall open. One look at Alex's red, puffy eyes and tear-ravaged face and Lisa's *How are you this morning* greeting died in her throat. Instead, she dried her hands, hurried to the door, and gathered Alex in her arms. "We're going to fix this." A listless shrug was all the answer she received.

Lisa pulled away and cupped Alex's shoulders in her hands. "Look at me." She continued when Alex's watery gaze lifted to her own. "I know you're hurt and discouraged, but this is a process, Alex. No matter how much we want to change...or want someone else to change, we have to give God time to work out the kinks. Don't give up. It's only been a week." She gave her friend's shoulders a little shake. "I still think God has a plan."

"Yeah, He keeps telling me the same thing, but..." Alex's voice was toneless, accented by the fresh tears welling in her eyes. She pulled out of Lisa's grasp and swiped the sleeve of her shirt across her eyes. "Sorry, I thought I was all cried out. I didn't think there was this much extra water in the human body."

"Don't apologize to me. We've all been there." She turned back to the coffeepot. "Dave's on the phone in his office, and I was fixing him coffee. You want some? I've got a new favorite creamer, and I'm willing to share."

"Whatever."

Lisa ignored the ambiguous answer and poured three cups. She doctored two with enough cream and sugar to sweeten even the gloomiest morning and handed one to Alex. "Follow me. These back halls are like a maze. Wouldn't do for you to get lost." The joke fell flat as Alex took the cup with downcast eyes and not even the hint of a smile. Lisa headed down the hall and heard Alex shuffling along behind her. *Father, please give us the wisdom we need to help these two work this out. I don't believe in divorce...* Her prayer trailed off. They were sort of already divorced. She turned a mental eye up and continued her prayer. *I'm glad You're smarter than I am because this whole thing is beyond confusing. I told her You have a plan, and I believe that. Please help us find it.*

"WE'RE HERE."

Dave looked up from his desk at the sound of Lisa's voice. His wife's lips formed two silent words before she stepped aside to allow Alex to enter. *It's bad.*

Alex stepped through the door, and Dave's heart broke for the woman. Her whole posture spoke of defeat. If Hunter had been standing in front of him in this instant, Dave would have kicked his butt. He accepted his cup of black coffee from Lisa who then sat in one of the visitor chairs. Alex continued to stand just inside the room. Dave frowned. She almost looked...afraid.

"Alex."

She started at the word but finally looked his way. He motioned to the other chair in front of his desk. "Would you like to sit?"

Alex moved into the room. She sat on the edge of the chair, holding her coffee in both hands and staring into the depths of the cup as if the answers to all of her problems might be found there if she looked hard enough.

Dave decided to go with it. "See anything interesting floating around in there?"

Alex's lips tipped up at the corners in a tiny smile that didn't reach her eyes. "Other than the little guy standing on a bubble holding a sign that says 'You're an idiot'"? She set the cup on the edge of the desk. "But then I already knew that."

Lisa reached over and rubbed Alex's arm.

Dave leaned forward. "Why do you think that?"

"Because I bought it again. Because I got my hopes up again. Because I'm the one who went home empty-handed. Again." Her lips tightened into a straight line, and her jaw worked as she swallowed. "Tell me. Who's the bigger fool? The person who spins the same lie month after month, year after year, or the person who continues to believe it."

"Walk me through it," Dave said.

Alex began with the birth of a set of twins and a moment of bonding she'd shared with Hunter. "He talked about Moses. How you'd helped him see some unflattering similarities."

Dave nodded and made some notes on a pad, gratified to know that Hunter had listened to that story.

"He apologized and asked me to meet him for dinner.

Said he had some ideas on how to *fix* things." Alex stood and paced to the door and back. "Then I guess he found something more important to do." She wrapped her arms around herself. "Just like always."

Dave shared a look with his wife and read the urge to throttle Hunter Conklin in her expression. Two against one...they could take him.

"I don't know what to do anymore." Alex's words were a mournful whisper. "I keep praying. God says He has a plan, but I can't see the next step." She sat down and looked from Lisa to Dave. "I know God takes marriage vows very seriously. I know that there are very narrow parameters for divorce." She motioned to Dave. "If I were on the other side of that desk, looking at a normal married woman, and those parameters hadn't been met, I'd counsel her to do what she could to fix what was broken. But this isn't a normal situation. We're already divorced. Maybe trying to fix that is doing the right thing for the wrong reasons."

"What do you mean?" Lisa asked.

Alex stood again, brushed her hair out of her face, and circled the room. "I have a friend from junior high. She has a sister, but her parents always wanted a son. Thirty years ago, the parents got a call in the middle of the night from a friend. He knew a woman who was about to take her infant son to a shelter because she couldn't care for him. If they acted fast, they could adopt this boy and have the son they'd always wanted." Alex continued to walk as she talked. "So here's this baby, and his choices are an orphanage or them. My friend's parents didn't think twice much less pray about it. The Bible commands us to care for orphans, right? They went and picked that child up that night and brought him home. The adoption was legal six months later. That boy has been nothing but trouble since he learned how to walk.

Years of counseling, jail time, living on the street. But how can you fault the parents? They did what they thought was right. They did the Christian thing. Would things have been different if they'd waited? Did God maybe have better parents in the wings, and they got in God's way? They're never going to have the answer to those questions."

Alex came back to the desk and drank deeply of her cold coffee. "So here are my questions. Hunter and I both had a call on our lives to do something special for God. Were we wrong in trying to combine those callings? Or did we go wrong in getting back together for the sake of our unborn babies? Or is it now that we're trying to do the right thing for the wrong reason? Maybe God had a purpose in bringing that divorce filing to light when He did. Maybe our trying to get back together...trying to squish our misshaped marriage into a mold that's never worked because that's what everyone expects us to do, is the right thing for the wrong reasons." She sat and put her head in her hands. "I don't even know if that makes sense to anyone but me. I just know that I can't continue to live like this."

"WHAT WERE YOU THINKING?"

Hunter glanced up, closed his eyes, and pinched the bridge of his nose.

Dave advanced into the room and leaned on the older man's desk with both hands. "I just left your wife sobbing in my office. She's ready to kick you to the curb." He stopped when he saw Hunter flinch under the words, but this wasn't the time for kid gloves. "I gotta tell you, I'm right there behind her." He straightened. "I thought you wanted to fix your marriage."

"I do."

"You have a poor way of showing it."

"I...it..." Hunter slouched back into his chair. "I know how it looks." He picked up his phone and tossed it to Dave. "Look at the call log. I bet I've called or messaged Alex a hundred times in the last sixteen hours. She won't take my calls, won't let me explain—"

"You have an explanation?"

Hunter pulled his hands down the length of his face. "Maybe more reason than explanation. If she'd just listen."

Dave laid the phone on the desk and took a seat. The man didn't look much better than his wife. Dark circles under his eyes, a day's worth of scruff on his normally clean-shaven face. Maybe there was more to the story than a forgotten dinner. "Tell me what happened." He listened as Hunter recounted the last twenty-four hours. As the story unfolded, Dave's attitude softened. Problem was, he could see it. He'd lived it more times than he could count. He didn't necessarily buy into the missed dinner thing, but he could see where a man in the habit of putting everything and anything in front of the needs of his wife could lose his best intentions in the face of a chaotic day. When Hunter finished, both men sat in silence for a few moments.

"I've had days like that," Dave admitted.

When Hunter looked up, his hopeless expression wasn't so rough around the edges. "I want to make it up to her, but she won't listen."

"Good thing your counselor is also your friend. I'm not going to lie to you. This process took some serious damage last night, but I think we can fix it." Dave reached across the desk and retrieved Hunter's cell phone. He swiped open an app and held it up for Hunter to see. "See this. This thing will store appointments for you and remind you of them.

You need to learn how to use it. If you'd called Alex with an apology beforehand and an offer to move your date, you'd be dealing with moderate disappointment instead of angry frustration. Does Alex know the family of the guy in the accident?"

Hunter nodded.

Dave sat back down and braced one leg across the other. "You know, you could have taken her with you. You'd have had some time alone in the car and, even if dinner had needed to be delayed, the night wouldn't have been a total bust."

"It never crossed my mind," Hunter admitted.

"Beyond that, if you had called her and explained, do you think she'd have given you grief for attending to a legitimate emergency?"

Hunter straightened, irritation stained his face. "Of course not. Alex is as dedicated to our congregation as I am. She's upset with me, but she's not petty."

Dave held out a hand. "Down boy. You just made my point for me. She isn't unreasonable, just hurt. We can fix the hurt, but"—he met Hunter's gaze and held it steady—"I don't think we can patch it twice in the same spot. The next time you stand her up might be the last time."

"I'm an idiot."

Dave decided to cut him some slack. "Not an idiot. But you have to realize that you can't do things the way you've always done them and expect a different result. You're learning to exercise a whole new muscle group, and there's bound to be some pain involved. I'll talk to Lisa, Lisa will talk to Alex. The fact that you're hiring an assistant to take over some of the duties should earn you a few brownie points."

Hunter looked visibly relieved. "Tell her I'm sorry. Tell

her I love her. Ask her to forgive me. Set up a time for dinner any night this week other than tonight, and I'll be there."

Dave stood and gave the time out signal. "Whoa, I'm not your social secretary. We'll make sure she understands the circumstances that led to last night's debacle. You need to give her some time to think. We'll advise her to take your call tomorrow so you can offer your own apology. The rest is on you." Dave stood and crossed to the door. He turned with his hand on the knob and narrowed his eyes at Hunter. "You don't get a lot of do-overs in life. Don't screw this one up."

HUNTER WATCHED THE DOOR CLOSE, a sigh of relief and a prayer of gratitude on his lips. "Father, thank You for second chances. You've allowed me to see where I've fallen short. With Levi's help, You've given me the means to begin to fix it. I love my wife so much. If You could just please soften her heart a little, I won't mess this up again."

As the words of his prayer died away, Hunter propped his elbow on the desk and put his chin in his hand while the nails of the other hand tapped the desk in a thoughtful rhythm. He could call tomorrow and offer his own apology, ask Alex out again and start along the road to reconciliation. And he would, but he wanted a bigger plan. Something Alex would never dream of, something special that the *old Hunter* would never have come up with. The cruise was a good start, but...

The idea formed so hard and fast in his head that it almost knocked him out of his chair. He grabbed a pad of paper and started making notes. When he finished, he stared at it. The timing worked, but only if he had some help from a lot of really good people. People he had access to, he reminded himself.

He picked up the phone, called the travel agent, and booked the Hawaiian cruise she had searched out for him. Was it a lack of faith that he bought the travel insurance just in case Alex didn't forgive him? He hoped not. Next he dialed his sons. They'd wanted to do something special for his and Alex's anniversary...he would give them that chance.

FIFTEEN

Alex crumbled her orange cranberry muffin Thursday morning. She stared around Ground Zero, refusing to meet Lisa Sisko's gaze. Garfield's little coffee shop was decorated in the pretty pastels of spring. A single tulip in a small cut glass vase rested on each of the half dozen tables. The cookies in the display case boasted Easter egg themed frosting. The small display window contained logo printed cups nestled in multicolored Easter grass. An involuntary shudder ran down Alex's spine. She hated Easter grass. It was always such a sticky mess by the end of the day. She pulled herself back to the present and glanced at Lisa. "You're kidding me, right?"

"Nope."

"So he lies to me again. He blows me off again. And because he convinces Dave how sorry he is, I'm just supposed to suck it up, put a happy face on my feelings, and dive in for another serving." Alex's fork finished the mutilation of the muffin. "Of all the man-serving, take up for each other... Why am I surprised that Dave would take Hunter's side? Is there some"—she waved the fork in the air—"some fraternal handbook someplace that all ordained men take an oath of office on? Vows never to violate the sacred office by seriously considering that one of the brethren might actually be wrong. It's just another good-old-boys' club."

Lisa's eyes went round, and sparks of indignation and anger ignited in their depths. She sat back and crossed her arms. Alex cringed beneath the hurt she'd just caused.

"There was a time I might have agreed with you on that," Lisa said, her voice controlled. "My father was a card-carrying member of that club. But you're wrong about Dave. If you can't see through your anger to that reality..." Lisa folded her napkin around the remains of her own muffin, her actions brisk, her expression taut, and tossed her long black hair over her shoulder. "If that's the way you really feel, then regardless of how much we both love you, neither of us can help you." She prepared to stand. "Call me when you come to your senses."

Alex stopped Lisa's exit with a hand on her wrist. "I'm sorry. That was unfair and uncalled for. You guys are both going above and beyond." When Lisa settled back into her seat, Alex released her. "I'm just..." She looked away, searched for a word, and came up empty. "I don't know what I am. Fed up...done...over it...scared." The last word came out as a whisper. She closed her eyes and explored that final possibility.

"Scared of what," Lisa asked.

"I'm scared of being alone. I'm scared of missing God. I'm scared that I'll lose my kids if I do what's best for me. I'm scared that things won't ever change." Her shoulders sagged, and tears brimmed in her eyes. "I'm scared that if things do change, I won't be enough to hold my husband's attention, and this will all have been for nothing."

Lisa tilted her head. Compassion replaced the irritation

of a moment before. "Where do you think all those negative feelings are coming from?"

Alex dabbed at her eyes with a crumpled napkin and gave a disconsolate shrug. It was a rhetorical question, since they both knew the answer.

Lisa leaned forward, took Alex's hand, and pulled her in until their foreheads touched across the small table. "Father, we come against this hurt and Satan's lies in the name of Your son, Jesus," she whispered for Alex's ears alone. "Your word says that You didn't give us the spirit of fear but of a sound mind. Your word reminds us that Satan is the father of lies and cannot speak the truth. When the devil says no, Your word is yes. When the devil says we aren't enough, Your word says we are more than enough. Father, we need clarity and holy determination in fighting this battle. We claim those things. We refuse to settle for less."

"Look," Lisa said as she straightened. "You remember what we talked about that first night?"

"We talked about a lot."

"Yes, we did. But, I remember talking specifically about the ministry being a people oriented calling. How we have to be serious about guarding our time with our family while understanding that emergencies happen."

Alex nodded.

"This wasn't about forgetting you. It was about Hunter doing what comes naturally for Hunter. It's unfortunate that his first reaction overrode his good intentions. We're all working to change that, Hunter included." Lisa paused. "You want Hunter to give, but you need to give a little too. If he'd called you to explain about the accident, would you have asked him not to go?"

"Of course not," Alex said. "When people are hurt or in trouble, the presence of a pastor is essential."

"Well, there you go." Lisa squeezed Alex's hand before letting it go. "Give him another chance. Take his call tonight and let him explain. There are a lot of little pieces that added up to the sum total of Hunter's day on Tuesday. I promise you are going to like some of them."

There was that promise again. Alex searched her friend's face. "Which parts am I going to like?"

Lisa finished picking up her trash. "Not my story to tell. Now, if you're good, I need to get over to the school. I have a conference with the principal. The twins traded places for a class last week and got caught."

Alex laughed. "I remember those days. Go easy on them. You'll miss those shenanigans once they outgrow them."

"From your mouth to God's ears...the outgrowing part anyway," Lisa tossed the remark over her shoulder as she walked from the building.

Alex sat for a few more minutes, pondering everything Lisa had said. Hunter must have something positive in the works. He'd mentioned it. Lisa and Dave had mentioned it. Hope stirred, but Alex refused to give it much room to grow. She'd take Hunter's call, she'd listen to what he had to say, but she wouldn't get her hopes up. So many of Hunter's promises had turned out to be oceanfront property in Kansas...AKA nonexistent. She piled up her own trash and left Ground Zero. Despite her protests to the contrary, the slightest of smiles replaced the morning's tears. She told herself that it had nothing to do with Hunter and everything to do with her impending visit with Mac and the babies.

HUNTER WAITED until midafternoon on Thursday to call his wife. Even then, he held the phone and stared at it for several seconds before punching in her number. He'd spoken to his sons yesterday. They were on board with his plans, but like him, hadn't a clue where to start. He'd need the help of Alex's friends, and he worried that he wouldn't get it. His stomach churned at the thought. He'd have to tell them everything...the very people he'd specifically told Alex not to tell were the ones he'd have to bare the truth to. His grand surprise was doomed to failure without them. He blew out a breath, and his hand tightened around the phone. That bridge needed to be crossed later. If he couldn't get Alex to accept his apology and explanation, he wouldn't need her friends.

He swiped the phone and dialed. Hunter's heart sank after the fifth ring. Was he out of chances? *Please, God, don't let me be out of chances.*

"Hello, Hunter."

"Hey, Alex." Two thoughts flashed through Hunter's mind in the time it took to swallow. She'd answered knowing it was him. She didn't necessarily sound thrilled, but she didn't sound angry.

"Are you there?"

"Yes, sorry. I have a lot on my mind."

Alex's sigh was harsh over the phone. "If you're busy—"

"You," he said hastily. "I have the most beautiful woman in the world on my mind." This time it was Hunter's turn to wait for a response.

"That's...sweet."

Hunter smiled. He could tell by the tone of Alex's voice that he'd flustered her. It was a start he could live with.

"And true," he said. "Would that beautiful woman allow me to buy her dinner tonight?"

"Sure...if you want."

Her lack of enthusiasm put a dent in his earlier assessment. He wondered how much of her agreement was her willingness to give him another chance and how much was due to Lisa and Dave's urging. "I know I messed up, sweetheart. I don't deserve a second...hundredth chance, but I want to explain. I want you to know how much I love you. I miss you." Hunter waited, dangerously close to begging. A man shouldn't have to beg his wife for attention.

Neither should a wife have to beg for her husband's.

Hunter closed his eyes at the soft rebuke. He was hearing marital advice from more than just Dave Sisko these days. His heavenly Father seemed to have strong views on the subject of marriage now that Hunter was taking the time to listen.

"Where?"

"I can pick you up...like a real date."

"Just tell me where. If you want it to be a real date, try showing up."

Her comment rankled. Hunter made a conscious effort to ignore it. He'd earned it. He looked at his watch—four p.m. "In two hours at Lizzy's. I was in there for lunch, and the air was thick with cinnamon. We could share a piece of her apple pie with ice cream after our meal." He held his breath, not at all ashamed that he'd used Alex's favorite dessert as an enticement.

"I'll see you there."

The phone went dead in his hand. Hunter slipped it away, got his office printer busy on some documents he needed, and went to the Sunday school supply room to see if he could find a piece of ribbon. He wanted a bow around tonight's surprise.

Ninety minutes later, a full thirty minutes early, Hunter slid into a booth at Lizzy's Diner and laid the ribbon-tied papers next to his plate. Not a chance he was missing this appointment. He pulled his phone from a pocket and set it to vibrate. He'd watch the screen until Alex showed up, but he'd put the phone away once she got there. He wanted no distractions. *Father, this is important to me. I get the feeling that You feel the same. Can You please just keep everyone healthy and happy for a couple of hours?*

The phone rang before he could even say amen. A glance at the screen had his heart rate kicking up. Charlene Hubbard, Alex's friend since college.

"Charley, thanks for returning my call."

"What can I do for you?"

The clipped tone of her response opened an emptiness in the pit of Hunter's stomach that had nothing to do with hunger. How much had Alex told them? Didn't matter. His plan was sunk before it sailed unless Alex's friends got on board. "I need your help. I'm working on a surprise for Alex. Something that will, I hope, show her how much she means to me. Time is short...two weeks short. I know you're her friend. I know since I've hurt your friend, you don't have a lot of reason to help me, but—"

"What do you need?"

Hunter gave a quick sigh of relief. He'd half expected her to turn him down flat. "I know this is short notice, but I need to meet with all of you Saturday morning if you can."

"All of us?"

"You, Syd, Jesse, Randy. We can leave Mac out of this, since she just had the babies."

"Oh...I don't think so."

His heart sank to his toes. "Charley, please. You have no idea how important this is." He frowned when Charley laughed.

"No, you misunderstood. We'll help you, but Mac will kill us if we leave her out. What do you have in mind?"

Hunter paused when he saw Alex's car slide into a parking space across the street. "I can't explain now. Can you call the others? I'll call you tomorrow if that's OK, and we can discuss time and place." He smiled at Alex as she came through the door.

"That's fine," Charley said. "You know we'll all die of suspense between now and Saturday, right?"

"It's all good. No reason for anybody to die," Hunter promised. "I gotta go." He swiped the call closed and put the phone in his pocket just as Alex took her seat. She narrowed her eyes.

"Something important?"

"Nothing that won't wait," Hunter told her. He relaxed, only admitting, now that they were at the same table, how much he'd feared that she wouldn't come. That she'd stay away to punish him.

You know better.

He did. There wasn't a petty bone in Alex's body. He drank in the sight of her. She was more beautiful now than when he'd married her. She'd been lovely then, of course, but more than two decades of living and ministry had added character, strength, and expression to her face that the twenty-something girl he'd fallen in love with hadn't possessed. How had he ever taken this woman for granted?

"You look amazing."

"Thanks, I..."

Before she could complete her thought, the server approached for their orders. They ordered the chicken fried steak dinner and sweet tea. Hunter smiled at his wife when the waitress departed. "We've been sucked into each other's habits."

"I guess we have," Alex agreed. "Before I met you, I hadn't had a chicken fried steak in years. Too many calories. Us short girls have to be careful when we're looking for that special someone. Not that I...I mean, I hope I haven't let myself go. That's not why—"

He took her hand. "Amazing," he repeated and brought her hand to his lips. "There's not a single piece of you I don't love. I mean...I don't..." They both dissolved in laughter as the tension at the table lightened.

"You'll never be fat. That's what I was trying to say," Hunter told her. The waitress came back with their tea and salads. Hunter waited while she exchanged a few words with Alex, grateful for the added time to organize what he needed to say. Once the young woman scooted to the next table, he met his wife's eyes.

"I'm sorry about Tuesday. So much went wrong that day."

Alex sipped her tea. "Lisa told me about Missy and Eric. Of course you had to go."

"I did, but that was only a small part of a day gone haywire from the beginning." He told her about the early morning issues with the church plumbing and added some detail to the Missy and Eric saga. "On top of all of that, I had an emergency meeting with someone I'm very excited for you to meet."

"Oh?"

Hunter lifted the roll of papers, secured with a bright yellow ribbon. *Father, please let her see the possibilities.* He handed them across the table. "Take a look and tell me what you think."

Alex accepted the papers with a puzzled look, pulled the ribbon loose, and flattened them in front of her. Hunter watched as she read Levi's resume, loving the little frown of confusion that gathered between her brows.

Alex looked up. "I don't understand. I've heard Sean mention Levi but why do you want me to meet him?"

"I'm pretty sure he's the answer to your prayers."

"My prayers?"

Hunter took her hand, twined her fingers in his. "Our prayers. Levi is on a mission trip. He left yesterday morning, which was why it was important that I meet with him Tuesday night. When he gets back"—Hunter tugged her hand until she met his gaze—"he'll be taking the newly created position of assistant pastor at Grace Community." He grinned when Alex's eyes went wide. "If you can bear with me until Levi gets back, we're going to do everything we can to make sure that you, and my family, are never neglected again.

SIXTEEN

Seven days later, Alex slipped her key into the lock of the family home for the first time in more than two weeks. The silence that greeted her felt almost as stuffy as the air. She was used to being alone in the house, coming and going from this place by herself, but this was different. The atmosphere carried an emptiness that nearly broke Alex's heart. She believed that homes had a soul. Oh, not the eternal ones God gave to humans, but something that breathed life and safety to the people that lived between the walls.

She stepped across the threshold and patted the door frame. "It's going to be OK," she whispered to whatever was listening. "I won't be gone much longer." The words brought a smile. After last week's debacle, she'd worried that her next trip here would be to pack the rest of her belongings. So much had changed between then and now.

Hunter was still Hunter, busy and often distracted. But Alex found she could ignore some of that now that he took the time to call her every day to see how she was and what she was doing. The hope that she'd refused to give place to was growing despite her efforts to hold it to a minimum.

They'd had lunch with the boys Sunday afternoon after morning service, their first time together as a family since she'd moved out. She'd expected some tension around the table, but instead the meal had resonated with laughter. She'd intercepted several strange looks between father and sons and wondered briefly what was behind them. But when talk turned to Sean's upcoming transfer to Oregon at the start of the next school year...

Oregon... That was so far from home. She swallowed back the emotions that threatened to swamp her. He wouldn't leave until mid-August. Deep in her heart, Alex had accepted that this was God's path for her son. She'd prayed for God's will in the lives of both of her boys since the day they were born. She could hardly pitch a fit when that will took them someplace new. A single tear escaped to roll down her cheek. Well...maybe just a little fit.

With a deep breath, she shook away the mulligrubs. It would work out. She'd always wanted to visit the Oregon Coast. With Sean living there for the next two years, what better justification for the trip. Maybe Hunter would go with her.

Baby steps, she cautioned herself. It felt like he was offering the moon this week, but the stars were still a long way out of reach.

She looked down the hall, almost giving in to the desire to pack up another batch of clothes or a few more books, but she resisted. Their twenty-third anniversary was eight days away, the projected end to their separation just a few days after that. She'd be home for good by then.

Please, Father.

Alex continued into the kitchen. She needed a recipe

for the dinner she was preparing for Hunter tonight. The lemon-blueberry cheesecake recipe Callie Stillman had given her had become one of Hunter's favorites and would make the perfect end to the dinner she'd planned.

The kitchen, always the hub of her home, seemed even more desolate than the hallway had. It was neat—Hunter wasn't a slob—but there was a layer of dust that wouldn't have been there if Alex were home. She swiped a finger along the top of the coffeemaker and shuddered. She went to the drawer, snapped up a dish towel, and wiped it until it gleamed. She turned to look for other targets and laughed at herself. If she cleaned the kitchen, she'd end up cleaning the whole house. If she cleaned the house, she could kiss her plans for dinner good-bye. She folded the cloth and hung it over the handle of the oven. With her hands on her hips, she turned in a small circle and spoke aloud. "I promise to get everything spic and span in a few days." It could have been her imagination, but something in the atmosphere shifted. "Good." Alex went to her recipe box, flipped through the cards, and found the one she wanted. A quick look confirmed that she'd need to go to the store before going back to the apartment. She made her way back out to the front porch and closed and locked the door. She put her hand on the wood just below the small, decorative window. *Father, thank You for this place and all You've blessed me with. Keep it safe for my return.*

HUNTER SAT at his desk with his phone to his ear while he drummed the fingers of his other hand on the edge of his desk. "Syd's daughter? You sure she's up for this sort of thing?"

"Ginny does amazing work," Charley told him.

"Well, I asked for your help. I'm not in a position to second-guess you at this point. We only have eight more days to make this happen."

"We're getting there," Charley said. "I've talked to Melanie Mason. You know her?"

"She owns the bakery."

"That's right. She's in, and she has a friend who has a friend who might be willing to help us. You still want pink?"

"Yes."

"Hunter, you know these are going to cost you a small fortune, right?"

"I don't care." He shifted to lean on the desk. "They're her favorite. I'm pretty sure she thinks I don't know that."

"But, twenty-three dozen—"

"A dozen for every year she's put up with me. She loves them, and she'll have them."

"You know they're poisonous, right?"

"We aren't planning to eat them."

"Whatever. The people I've talked to so far say they haven't had any in their stores for ten years." Charley's sigh carried over the phone. "I love that you're doing this for her. I love that you're letting us help, so I'll stop complaining. I'll talk to Melanie's friend's friend and get back with you. Melanie needs an answer there before she can finalize her plans."

"Understood. I appreciate everything you ladies are doing."

Charley laughed. "Don't appreciate us too much. We haven't pulled it together yet."

"But I know you will. The boys are making headway on their part as well. Transportation has been secured and

Sean is tugging on a lead. We all just need to stay focused."

"Yeah, and you just need to keep your checkbook handy."

The phone went dead in Hunter's hand, and he grinned down at it. They were going to pull this off. Alex and he would have a new beginning complete with all the things his bride had missed out on the first time around.

A sudden longing for Alex washed over him. She was cooking dinner for him tonight, but he needed to hear her voice now. He punched in her number. Contentment washed over him when she answered on the first ring.

"Hey, gorgeous. What are you up to today?"

"Oh, cooking dinner for some guy I know. How about you?"

The humor in Alex's voice made him smile. Such a drastic change from a week ago. "I just needed to hear your voice," he answered honestly. "I can't wait to see you. Is there anything you need me to bring tonight? I can stop by the store on my way."

"Just your appetite. I'm making your favorite."

Hunter's mouth started to water. "The chicken in the white wine sauce?"

"Got it in one. You know that sauce won't keep. Don't be late."

"Not on your life," Hunter promised.

ALEX, her hands buried to the wrists in bread dough, hummed a little tune while she kneaded. The apartment's tiny kitchen looked like a war zone in the midst of a battle. Dishes awaited her attention in the sink. Cutting boards lined the counter—chicken on one, veggies on another, and a third just-in-case. Spice bottles formed a haphazard line along the windowsill, soldiers awaiting their call to action.

She grinned as she patted the dough, spread a clean towel over the top, and used her arm to brush damp hair from her forehead. Cooking was one of her favorite things. She loved prowling through the many cookbooks in her collection for new and interesting ideas. She liked to experiment, and God had blessed her with two bottomless and very willing guinea pigs. Before they'd gone off to school, Sean and Benjamin had spent at least one evening a week in the kitchen with Mom, setting up menus. In addition to the planning, they'd never considered it *sissy* to scrub up their hands and pitch in. Alex had years of precious memories of herself and the boys preparing meals. Starting with identical step-stools pulled up to the counter so her toddlers could decorate cookies all the way to high school and more complicated dishes that often surprised all of them.

And Hunter? Well, he ate for fuel, not taste, more often than not, and since most of his meals ended up reheated in the microwave at some ungodly hour of the evening, he seldom expressed any preference.

But tonight? Tonight's dinner would encompass all of Hunter's favorites. Chicken with a white wine sauce served over rice, a Caesar salad with her special homemade dressing, fresh dinner rolls, and cheesecake for dessert. A busy afternoon in the kitchen for sure, but a labor of love. She checked the clock. The timing had to be exact or the rolls would be cold, the rice would be a pile of sticky mush, and the sauce would separate into a lumpy mess.

All the prep work was done. She had two hours to let the dough rise, clean the kitchen, and make herself presentable before the can't-leave-the-kitchen stage kicked in. She loaded the dishwasher and scrubbed the sink while the cheesecake finished baking. Once it was out of the oven, she'd have some time to spend on herself. A long soak in a hot bubble bath sounded almost as good as tonight's menu. After a final look at the kitchen, she went to get ready for her husband. Her friends weren't here to help make her beautiful, but she figured she could manage this one on her own.

HUNTER TURNED the light out in his office. His phone rang just as he reached for the door.

"Hello."

"Dad, I've got good news. My friend's uncle?"

"Yes."

"I just managed to catch him. He was hesitant at first, but once I explained what we were doing he softened up. Man, this has got to be a total God thing! They had a cancellation thirty minutes before I called. He's willing to bump us to the top of the waiting list, but you have to sign the papers and give him a deposit tonight."

Hunter stopped in the doorway. "What time?"

"As soon as you can get there. It's about four miles south of Highway 9 and Harrah. He says you can't miss the sign. Dad, I looked up the website, Mom will love it."

Hunter blew out a breath. He was supposed to be at Alex's in less than an hour. Her final admonition rang in his ears. *Don't be late.* He calculated the time to make the trip, do a walk-through, and get back to town. Ninety minutes any way he sliced it.

"Dad?"

"Just trying to work the timing out in my head, son. Tomorrow would be better."

"If he doesn't hear back from me in ten minutes he's calling the next name on his list."

Hunter's stomach lodged someplace around the bottom of his throat, and a cold sweat broke out on his forehead. This was not going to go well, but he didn't have a choice. "OK, call him, tell him I'm on my way." He ended the call and dialed Alex's phone.

"I hope you worked up an appetite," Alex said.

The carefree tone in his wife's voice robbed Hunter of his own for a second. He cleared his throat. "I did, but I've got a small problem."

Silence greeted his announcement.

"Something urgent has come up, and I'm going to be about an hour late. Can you put dinner on hold?"

"Hunter—"

"I know, sweetheart, but I can't get out of this. It might not even be an hour. I promise to be there just as soon as I can."

"Church business?"

The question was clipped.

"No."

"Is someone in the hospital?"

"Nothing like that."

"Then what is it?" she asked, her tone growing more impatient with each word. "What's so important that all the work I've put into tonight's dinner is pointless."

"Sweetheart, it wasn't pointless." What could he say? The truth was an impossibility if he wanted to keep his surprise. His surprise was trashed if he screwed up tonight's plans. "Look, I can't explain it right now. You're going to have to trust me and know that I love you."

The line went dead in his hands.

ALEX SWIPED THE CALL CLOSED. It took all of her willpower not to throw the phone down the garbage disposal when it rang and Hunter's number flashed on the display.

"Trust him? Know that he loves me?" She looked around the apartment. The coffee table was set with linen and candles. Pots simmered on the stove. A dozen fresh rolls were fifteen minutes from being browned to perfection. Her gaze dropped to her outfit. She'd spent almost an hour on clothes, hair, and makeup. Tonight was supposed to be perfect.

How's that working for you?

"Shut up!" she hissed at the snarky little internal voice that snickered at her disappointment.

Alex marched to the oven, grabbed the pot holders, and yanked the pan of rolls from the oven. She lifted them one-by-one with tongs and dropped them into the garbage. "He loves me...he loves me not...he loves me...he loves me not." When the twelfth roll plopped in on *he loves me not,* Alex gave up her battle with heartbroken tears.

"Figures. The bread is smarter than I am. Fine." On the mumbled words, she opened the fridge, retrieved the salad and dumped it on top of the rolls. The action was oddly liberating, so much so that she anointed the lettuce and bread with her special salad dressing. Chicken, rice, and sauce followed. She grabbed up the cheesecake with every intention of sending it to the trash too. She froze in mid-step. She'd eat the whole thing before she threw it away. She didn't think it would come to that.

Alex set her dessert back on the counter and picked up her phone. She called Charley.

"Hello."

"It's Alex." No amount of self-control could reel in the tears that stained her voice.

"Hey...what's wrong?"

Alex swallowed. "I've got a 911 and a whole cheese-cake. I'm headed your way. Can you get the girls together?"

Charley's response was immediate. "Make it Mac's house, not mine. Give me thirty minutes."

Alex disconnected the call. Hunter would show up here when whatever *emergency* he was dealing with was dealt with. She refused to be home when he arrived.

SEVENTEEN

Hunter looked around his office at seven a.m. on Friday morning. Four uncertain faces looked back at him.

"It was pretty ugly," Randy said. "I don't think I've ever seen Alex quite so...upset. The word hardly fits, but it's the best I can come up with."

Jesse used a tiny straw to stir her coffee. "We convinced her to talk to Dave and Lisa Sisko before she did anything rash, but...man, Pastor." She paused to shove her glasses back into place. "I don't see this ending well."

"Not unless you tell her the truth," Syd said.

Hunter shook his head. "I'll be talking to Dave Sisko just as soon as we finish. I'll tell him the truth. Alex and I had been doing pretty well until last night. Hopefully he can convince her that an occasional step back is normal. Alex certainly knows I'm not perfect." *We're close, Father. I'm gonna need Your help.*

He met each of the women's gazes individually. "Seven days, ladies. Seven days and this will be over with." He took a deep breath and straightened. "Where are we?"

"Pretty solid," Randy answered. "Did you get what you were after last night?"

"I did. It's everything we were looking for and then some. I agree with Sean, that last minute cancellation was a God thing." He looked at Charley. "Flowers?"

"Twenty-three dozen vases of lily of the valley, pink and white mixed, will be delivered next Friday by noon."

"Perfect," Hunter said. He scribbled an address on a note pad and passed the paper to Charley. "This is where they need to go. I just hope they aren't delivered in vain."

"We're headed to the apartment as soon as we finish here." Charley smiled. "We have a cheesecake to finish off and a friend to comfort. We are going to do our best to bash you for being an unthoughtful ogre while convincing her to give you another chance."

"Thanks?"

"You should thank us," Syd said. "It's a woman thing. The harder we malign you, the more the love in her heart gets stirred up. She'll be taking up for you before we finish our cake and coffee."

Charley looked at him and laughed. "Relax. I see the reaction every day in domestic dispute cases. I know you have too. A couple is fighting, ready to go at each other, but don't let the cops barge into the middle of it. Nothing unites a couple faster than an outside influence taking one side or the other." She tilted her head and sent him an impish grin. "She'll be where you want her to be next Friday night, even if I have to handcuff her and haul her, kicking and screaming, in the back of my patrol car."

Jesse leaned forward and laid a sheet of paper on his desk. "Mac sent this. If it meets your approval, she can order it today."

Hunter studied the picture. He glanced at the price tag twice. "Two hundred and sixty-five dollars?"

"Express shipment," Jesse said. "Something we have no choice about right now. If you don't like it, say so. She can look at some others, but we need to finalize today."

"This is perfect." Hunter opened his desk drawer and took out his checkbook. "Charley, it's a lot of money. I don't mind paying—"

"We've talked about this." She put her hand on her gun, but the look she sent him was full of humor. "Don't make me hurt you."

Hunter raised his hands. "Yes, ma'am." He scribbled out a check, ripped it free, and passed it to Jesse. "Tell Mac I said thanks. Anything else?"

"Ginny is a go. I'll share the final details with Melanie so she can do what she does best." Charley waved at the picture on his desk. "We're good there and the flowers are coming. I think we're set. Anything else?"

He lifted a large manila envelope, opened it, and spread the contents across his desk. "This was waiting for me in the church's PO box this morning."

The ladies crowded around the desk.

Charley picked up a brightly colored brochure. "Wow."

"Would you look at that?" Jesse opened a folder and flipped through the contents. "This is some anniversary gift."

"I have a lot to make up for." Hunter's words echoed the sadness in his heart.

Randy met his gaze. "A twelve-day cruise island hopping in Hawaii..."

"Makes up for a whole heck of a lot," Syd finished.

They all looked up at the sound of a throat clearing. A very stern-faced Dave Sisko stood in the open doorway.

Hunter gathered up all the paperwork. "Ladies, I appreciate you bending your schedules to be here so early."

"Not a problem," Randy told him. "If Mac hadn't just given birth, we'd be sweating at the spa right about now."

Hunter acknowledged her statement with a nod. "If you need anything else, don't hesitate to call me, but for now"—he nodded at his new guest—"I'd appreciate some privacy."

The women trooped out, and Dave took their place. He sat, crossed his arms, and glared. "I just got off the phone with Alex." Dave stopped and gave Hunter a disbelieving shake of his head. "It's like you're trying to sabotage this whole thing."

"Trust me, that is not my intent."

"Then you need to tell me what's going on."

"Gladly...in fact, I need your help." Hunter laid the whole thing out for him.

When Dave left the office thirty minutes later, there was a smile of pure delight on his face.

ALEX BENT her head over her coffee cup. She had no energy this morning. She felt deflated, like a balloon pricked with a tiny pin. The air of hope and dreams and expectation that had kept her aloft for the last week leaked out of her almost imperceptibly.

"Hon, talk to us," Randy urged as she set her plate aside.

"There's nothing new to say," Alex said. "I know you guys came to prop me up, but I think I'm beyond propping."

"That's only true if you want it to be," Jesse said.

Alex shoved herself to her feet as the dam of restraint broke. "I don't get it." Her voice was harsh, the words coming out in a rush. "If things could get better in a week, they were. I mean, I almost had the old Hunter back."

"The old Hunter?" Syd asked.

Alex paced the room. "He wasn't always the workaholic, ignore-me man he is today." She faced her friends. "Don't get me wrong. Dedication is Hunter's middle name, but when we were first married, he was romantic and thoughtful."

You divorced him.

Alex turned away from her friends and considered the words from the spiteful little voice in her head. Yes, she had, or she'd started to, but that had been more about a difference of opinion than who her husband had been. An irreconcilable disagreement over her job that proved pointless with the impending birth of twins. Besides, her friends didn't know about the divorce...yet.

"Romantic and thoughtful," she repeated, more for herself than her friends. She turned. "He sent me flowers every week. When I was on bed rest for the last two months of my pregnancy, he cooked and cleaned and kept me company. When the boys were tiny, he was such an attentive father. Up for feedings every night. Pitching in around the house. Arranging an occasional sitter so we could have small outings."

"That's not the Hunter we all know and love," Randy said. "What happened?"

"I don't know," Alex answered. "After he accepted the promotion to senior pastor, he got busier and busier. It happened so gradually that I didn't even notice it at first. I just know that by the time the boys were in middle school, I was pretty much parenting on my own. I look back and think maybe I was just as much to blame as he was."

"How do you mean?" Charley asked.

"He was busy with a growing church, and I was busy with growing boys. We passed each other on the sidewalk as we came and went." She sighed and came back to her place on the couch. "We talked around the subject more times than I can count, but all we did was talk. We never took any steps to change things. It wasn't until the boys went away to college that I realized just how bad things had become."

Jesse leaned forward. "Like Hunter missing important dinners with his boys?"

Alex looked at her.

"I...umm...I was in your office one day. I heard part of an argument. Something about Sean bringing home a girl and Hunter not being there."

Alex could have sworn a small smile flittered around Jesse's lips.

"Not much of a father," Jesse said, "if you ask me."

Alex blinked. Had her friend just said that?

"Just...you know..." Jesse took off her glasses and cleaned them on the tail of her shirt. "What sort of dad refuses to compromise when it's important to his child?"

"Agreed," Charley said. "Jason would never neglect his daughter, no matter how demanding his schedule.

Someone knocked on the door of the apartment. Alex gave a tiny shake of her head as she went to see who it was. Something was up, and she didn't have a clue what it was. Last night, she'd almost felt betrayed by these women, so determined were they in their efforts to convince her to give Hunter another chance. Now today... She opened the door to a man holding a long box.

"Delivery for Alex Conklin."

Alex took the box. "Thanks. Wait right here."

"No need, ma'am. The sender included a nice tip for

me in the order." He touched the bill of his ball cap. "You have a good day now."

Alex watched him lope down the stairs before nudging the door closed with her foot. She turned to take the box to the bar and almost tripped over her four friends. She stepped around them, laid the box down, and removed the lid. Six blue roses rested in green tissue paper, a note nestled in the surrounding baby's breath.

"Oh..." Alex bent down to sniff.

"Bet those are from Hunter," Randy said.

"Typical man move." Jesse clasped her hands beneath her chin. "Please give me another chance," she said in a deepened voice.

Syd put a hand on Alex's shoulder. "Don't fall for it, girlfriend. The third time is not the charm."

"He'll just break your heart again," Charley agreed.

Alex straightened, pressed her lips together, and faced her friends with crossed arms.

"What's gotten into you guys?"

"What?" Randy asked.

"We love you," Jesse told her. "We don't like seeing you hurt."

Alex nodded, completely confused. She loved Hunter, and she was beyond angry with him. These women were only standing with her. *Right?* Wasn't that what friends did? Why did that frustrate her? "I appreciate that. I appreciate that you dropped everything and rushed to be with me last night and again this morning." She looked at the flowers. "But..."

Charley motioned to the roses. "Are you seriously thinking of putting yourself out there again?"

"I don't know," Alex answered honestly. "But I think I

need some time alone now, just me and God, to figure out what happens next."

"Are you sure?" Charley asked.

"Very."

Randy looked at her watch. "Shoot, Syd, it's almost nine, we're both going to be late."

The women put cups and plates in the sink, gathered their things, and filed out the door.

Alex watched them go, waiting for the door to close before she pulled the card from the bouquet of roses.

Alex, I used to send you roses a lot. Do you remember? I do. I'm not sure why I stopped. Always pink because I loved you. I still do. I know you're doubting that right now. I can't give you any explanation that would satisfy you, so I won't waste your time.

I sent you blue roses today because I'm told they have a special meaning. A gift of blue roses says the recipient is extraordinary and unique. You are both those things and so much more. Be extraordinary for me one more time. Our anniversary is in a week. I know that you're angry with me. I don't blame you, but give me that day. I won't bother you between now and then. Just give me that day before you make any decisions about our future. All my love, Hunter

Alex read the note twice. She looked at the flowers and read the note a third time. Tears spilled onto her cheeks, and her whispered prayer filled the room.

"Father, I'm so confused. All I've ever wanted was to be half of a whole. I've tried so hard to be a good wife, a good pastor's wife. I kept his house, I raised his children, I supported him on every step of his ministry and served right beside him. And now? Now we're in this impossible place, and I don't know what's right anymore. I thought that this time apart would help us find our way back to each other,

but instead it feels like so much wasted energy...my energy...
the last of my energy." Oh, those words hurt, even in prayer
to the God who knew her heart. The admission stole her
breath. She reached out to stroke the soft petals of the roses.

"I feel like I'm just beating the air. I know that You have
a plan for us. I know that You have a time for that plan. But
I need a hint...just a hint of where You're taking me and
what You want me to do. Ecclesiastes 3:1 tells us that there
is a time and a season for everything. Please show me."

*Yes, daughter. A time to weep and a time to laugh. A
time to love and a time to hate. A time to stand. When you
have done all you can do, stand. Be still, now, and know that
I am God.*

The combination of familiar verses drew Alex up, and
peace settled around her. *When you have done all you can
do.* She had, hadn't she? *Be still.* Take no action, rest. She
needed that for sure. *Wait.* Not said, but implied.

"Father, You ask some hard things. I hope it's worth it."
Words swam in her mind, and Alex ran for her phone and
the Bible app installed on it. "Every good gift...every good
gift." She mumbled the words as she typed. "There it is.
James 1:17. Every good gift and every perfect gift is from
above, and cometh down from the father of lights, with
whom there is no variableness, neither shadow of turning."
She closed the app and held her hand up to the spring light
streaming in through the window. Good gifts...gifts that
didn't change in the shifting lights or shadow. Gifts that
never varied from what was promised. She took a deep
breath and another look at the flowers.

"All right. I'll give him his week."

EIGHTEEN

Alex stretched as her eyes fluttered open from a melatonin-induced sleep on Friday morning, the tenth of May. The tenth of May. Her twenty-third wedding anniversary. She'd looked forward to and dreaded this day for a week. So much so that her little green bottle of melatonin had become her best friend. The stuff gave her weird dreams, but the dreams beat tossing and turning all night trying to figure out a future she had no handle on.

Give me that day.

She still had no clue what Hunter's words meant. No idea if he'd even remember that today was special.

Father, please... She slipped into the prayer as easily as pulling on her favorite slippers. Prayer had become her life-line this week, and, in return, peace had cushioned the worry like bubble wrap. Except at night, when she couldn't seem to muffle the little voices in her head. After lying awake till almost three Tuesday night, she'd made a deal with herself. If she wasn't asleep by midnight, melatonin.

True to his word, Hunter hadn't contacted her this

week. Beyond her single text to agree to his request, she hadn't talked to him either. She'd seen him at church on Sunday and Wednesday. He'd smiled, she'd nodded, but they'd exchanged no words. She shuffled in her fuzzy blue slippers to the kitchen and started the coffee. She looked out the window and frowned. It was a little odd, actually. She hadn't really talked to much of anyone in the last seven days. The boys had been busy with end-of-semester stuff, and her friends... Mac had the babies to take care of, and the others had husbands, kids, and jobs to occupy their time. Their silence shouldn't bother her. Except it did...a little. She was used to seeing them several times a week, with plenty of chitchat in between. This week, there'd been nothing. Even the six-way text that often zipped back and forth among them, often with nothing but inane chatter, had been silent.

"They have lives," she reminded herself as she stirred her first cup of coffee, "and you...?" Alex shook that off. *He wouldn't forget...would he?*

"Father, I'm trying not to think like that. Our time together this week has been precious and comforting. But You know me. Waiting is hard."

She wandered around the tiny apartment, restless, looking for something to do. Pointless really. It was just her, and she was pretty tidy. Her eyes landed on the vase with the remnants of the blue roses. She'd managed to keep them alive for a week, but they were ready for the trash. Alex sniffed them and made a face. Nothing smelled as sweet as fresh roses. Nothing stank as much as dead ones.

She gathered them up. "You have to go." She opened the door and jumped back with a little squeal. On the small landing sat a large vase with a dozen pink roses. She stepped to the banister and looked around. How long had they been here? It was barely eight. She turned back to stare at the flowers. The delicate petals, perfectly cupped and dotted with moisture, begged to be sniffed...and stroked. Alex dumped the wilted flowers in the small bin at the corner of the landing and scooped up the new ones. Her heart soared out from under the worry she'd done her best to ignore. They had to be from Hunter, right?

"Thank You, Father. Thank You." The words tumbled over each other as she carried them in, set them down, and removed the card.

Happy anniversary. I didn't want you to spend the day wondering if I remembered. I've arranged transportation for you tonight. You'll be picked up at five-thirty. I can't wait to see you. I love you. Hunter.

Alex buried her face in the fragrant blooms and inhaled before reaching for her phone. Hunter deserved a response. She dialed his number and waited. Lines gathered between her brows when his voicemail answered. What was up with that? He always answered his phone. She waited through the message, smiling when his deep voice came over the connection. *Sorry, I can't get to the phone just now. If this is urgent, please call Pastor Tillis at—*

She disconnected before the number repeated. That was new, Hunter directing calls to Levi. She tried the church phone.

"Pastor Levi."

Alex plopped down on one of the barstools. The morning was getting weirder by the second. Where was her husband? "Levi, this is..." She stopped to clear her throat. She hadn't met Levi. Would he know who she was? "This is Alex Conklin, Sean's mother...Pastor Hunter's wife. Is he available?"

"Good morning. Sorry, but Pastor is out running errands this morning. Can I take a message?"

The young man's voice carried a bright smile that charmed Alex straight to her toenails. She remembered the picture attached to the resume Hunter had given her. Shy good looks, wrapped in a bowtie, topped with a smile. She liked him already. "No, I'll call his cell."

"Well...see, that's the thing. He left it on his desk. I heard it ring just a few seconds ago."

"Oh...OK. Thanks."

"Don't mention it. I'll tell him you called."

Alex disconnected the call and stared at the phone. Out running errands...without his phone. What was the man up to?

She asked that question again when a knock sounded on her door at one p.m. Alex wiped sandwich crumbs from her mouth and hurried to answer. A delivery man stood there. He carried a large flat box adorned with a pink ribbon.

"Alex Conklin?"

"Yes."

He shifted the box into her arms. "This is for you." He was down the steps before she had a chance to respond.

Alex backed into the apartment, closed the door with her foot, put the box on the couch, and sat next to it. There was an envelope attached to the ribbon. Her hands shook as she pulled it free.

This isn't nearly as beautiful as you, but please wear it for me tonight.

Alex yanked the bow free and discarded the lid. She parted the layers of tissue paper and gasped. "Oh my..." The box contained a dress. *Not just any dress.* She lifted it free, stood, and held it up to the light. The cream-colored dress had a fitted waist, a lace bodice, and layers of chiffon on the skirt that would float around her knees as she walked. It was the most beautiful thing she'd ever seen.

"Hunter..." she breathed as tears blurred the dress. "What are you up to?"

She grabbed her phone and zipped off a text to her friends.

He sent me the most beautiful dress.

She received a series of smiley faces and thumbs up emoji's. She'd gotten the same when she told them about the roses. It was more than strange.

Two more deliveries came that afternoon. A pair of shoes with a matching bag and a set of pearls. The shoes and purse were silver and new. The pearls were from her jewelry box at home. They'd belonged to her mother and complimented the dress perfectly. In all this, she heard not a word from her husband or her friends.

Five-fifteen found Alex pacing the living room. She'd been right. The dress fit like it had been made for her, and the hem fluttered around her knees like a cloud as she walked. She'd put her hair up, taking extra time with her makeup. She no longer wondered if he'd forget, but she did wonder what would come next. She didn't have long to wait.

She heard a car door slam, followed by a knock. A man, dressed in a sharp black suit, a cap with a shiny black bill tucked under his arm, stood at the door.

"Mrs. Conklin?"

"Yes."

"I'm here to escort you. If you'd come with me." He motioned to a black limousine parked in the drive and held out his arm.

Alex turned and looked at the apartment. Something in

her heart told her that she wouldn't be back, not to stay anyway. She closed and locked the door.

The ride seemed endless as she watched the familiar scenery along Highway 9. Spring was taking hold of Oklahoma and everywhere she looked things were greening up with new life. The thought gave her a shiver. Was her marriage greening up as well? The limo took an unfamiliar turn and five minutes later stopped in front of a rustic building. Cars packed the parking lot and even though it was still a couple of hours before dusk, white fairy lights twinkled in the trees. Her confusion deepened when her sons, both in tuxedos, came out of the building. Benjamin opened the door for her, and Sean extended his hand to help her from the car.

"What's going—?"

"Shh..." they whispered in unison before stooping to kiss her cheeks.

Speechless, she allowed herself to be led through the double doors. Her eyes went round. Candlelight, soft music, and dozens of vases filled with white and pink flowers. Not just flowers, but her favorite flowers—lily of the valley. She blinked away sudden tears.

Charley, dressed in a dusty rose-colored dress in a similar style as hers came to her and thrust a bouquet of the same kinds of flowers into her hands. She steered her to an arched doorway and stopped. The first notes of the wedding march filled the building.

"Follow me," Charley whispered.

With one of her sons on each arm, Alex had no choice.

HUNTER, standing in the place of the groom, watched her

come. He smiled when her eyes met his, and even from this distance, he saw her swallow.

Dave Sisko took the place of officiating minister. Once his sons and his bride halted before Hunter, Dave asked the traditional question. "Who gives this woman in marriage?"

"We do," Sean and Benjamin said. They put her hand in Hunter's and retreated.

Dave motioned everyone into their seats. "This isn't your traditional wedding. Before we get started, the groom has something he'd like to say." He stepped to the side and gave Hunter the floor.

Hunter looked at Alex. "You're beautiful," he whispered. He tugged her hand and pulled her close. "Look at me." When she complied, he said, "No harm, no foul here, Alexandra. If this isn't what you want, if this isn't a step you feel comfortable with, say so now."

Alex bit her lip and looked into his eyes. Hunter watched while she searched his face, knew the instant her mind steadied. She nodded. He released her hand, pulled something from his pocket, and dropped to one knee. When he spoke, his voice boomed through the room.

"Alexandra, will you marry me...again?" He opened the small box in his hand to reveal a diamond ring to go with the plain wedding band Alex had worn on her ring finger for twenty-three years.

"Yes." Her answer was barely a whisper.

Hunter stood and took both of her hands. He looked out over the crowd. "She said yes. That's good, right?" Laughter rolled through the room.

Hunter looked at his wife. "Alex, I asked you that same question twenty-three years ago. I made promises to you twenty-three years ago. I haven't done the best job keeping those promises. Tonight, I'll make those promises again, and with God's help I'm going to do a better job." He blinked moisture from his eyes.

"I promise to be there for you, to put you first, to include you in everything I do. I promise to never take you for granted, never to leave you lonely, never to put you in a position that makes you feel less than cherished. I love you, and I plan to show you that you are my everything. On this I give you my word. "

ALEX HEARD THE WORDS, stunned at their meaning and the tears of sincerity she saw in her husband's eyes. She looked away for a second. She was surrounded by all the things two impetuous kids hadn't been able to afford all those years earlier. Music, flowers, candlelight, a beautiful dress, and friends to witness the moment. *He did all this, just for me.* She swallowed, knowing she was expected to say something but unable to think.

She looked at Hunter, her breath shallow in her chest. For a second, the world narrowed to a collection of tiny things, the green of his eyes, the smile that curved his mouth, and the scent of his cologne.

Daughter, say something.

Her father's words—and Alex didn't think she was imagining the humor in them—were all the prompting she needed. "Hunter, I've always loved you. Through the good and the bad, you've always had my heart. I give that to you fresh and new tonight. I promise to work beside you. I promise to lift you up in prayer every day. I promise to be the wife God created me to be...for you."

She closed her eyes as Hunter pulled her in for a kiss. The world melted, and time spun out until there was nothing but the two of them, nothing but the fresh new promises between them and a bright future ahead.

Dave Sisko coughed. "Hang on you two, let's not get ahead of ourselves. Business before pleasure." He straightened as the congregation's laughter faded.

"Dearly beloved..."

Alex didn't really hear the words. She lost everything in the eyes of the man she loved. When Dave pronounced them man and wife...again...she leaned into a kiss to seal their new promises. As she walked down the aisle on the arm of her husband, pausing every few steps for Ginny Marlin to snap a picture, she couldn't remember a time when she'd been happier.

Hunter leaned over to whisper in her ear. "You don't have any plans for the next couple of weeks, do you?"

Alex looked up at him. "Not really. Why?"

"I've got these tickets for a Hawaiian cruise in my pocket. You interested?"

Alex froze in mid-step.

"Close your mouth, sweetheart."

It took some effort, but Alex managed to drag her bottom jaw up from the carpet. "Hawaii?" The word was hardly more than a gasp.

"Twelve days worth." He maneuvered her out of the larger room and into a hall. "You have three hours to eat a slice of wedding cake and get packed." He paused in front of a door. "But first, there's one small piece of business we need to take care of." He threw it open to reveal Harrison Lake seated at a table with papers spread out in front of him.

"What...?"

"Vacate paperwork," Harrison told her as he pushed a pen into her hand. He pointed to a blank line just under

Hunter's signature. "Sign right there, and"—he made a motion in the air with his hand—"abracadabra, your divorce vanishes."

Alex squealed, scribbled her name on the dotted line, and launched herself into Hunter's arms. For the second time in ten minutes, she couldn't remember a time when she'd been happier.

EPILOGUE

Two years later

Alex clapped as two-year-old Aimee and Zachary blew out the candles on their birthday cakes. One chocolate and one white. The room was filled with people, and a table along the right side was stacked with presents.

Hunter put an arm around her waist and leaned over to kiss her hair. "Nice party."

Alex turned into his arms. "I remember a better one."

"You do?"

Alex smiled, boosted herself up on to her toes, and laid her lips on his. When she stepped back, electricity sizzled in the small space between them. "I do. Changed my life."

Hunter looked down at her and wiggled his eyebrows, a wicked smile on his face. "You packed?"

"I am." Their anniversary trip had become a yearly tradition. Last year, they'd traveled to Oregon to spend two weeks on the coast. They were leaving tomorrow on a two-week exploration of Australia. "I can't wait."

She embraced him again. *Changed my life* was an

understatement. The last two years had been as perfect as two imperfect people could make them. There were still days when one of them didn't get it right, but mostly—

"You two mind?" Mac stood to the side, a piece of cake in each hand. "You're stealing the thunder from a pair of toddlers."

They broke apart with a guilty grin.

"There's about to be a mess," Hunter said.

"Yep." Alex smiled up at him. She couldn't remember a time when she'd been happier. She'd experienced that a lot over the last two years. She looked around the room and took in the assembly with a smile. Life was often divided by before and after moments. She hadn't known, none of them had, that Mac's coming into their lives eight years ago would be one of those moments. Their sisterhood had been incomplete without her. Now...

Mac and Dane helped their twins with cake while Mac's grown son, Riley, stood by with a roll of paper towels and an indulgent *big brother* smile.

Randy bounced a new foster child on her hip while her husband Eli helped Astor add their gifts to the growing pile. This was their third foster, a six-month-old boy named Kyle. There was talk of adoption if the situation worked out.

Charley and Jason stood in a corner with their daughter, Kinsley, and Benjamin. They admired the new ring on her left hand while a recently married Sean and Ashley looked on.

Alex and Charley had been friends since college. She couldn't believe that, in a few months, they'd be in-laws. They'd share grandbabies, God willing. The thought sent tingles of anticipation up her spine.

Jesse, heavy with child, stood next to Garrett and debated which cake went with today's cravings. No twins there, but the baby was due in a matter of weeks, and Garrett was hovering with a watchful eye. Alex sent up a prayer that God would keep that baby safely in the oven till she and Hunter got back from their trip.

Syd and Mason sat with Syd's oldest daughter Sarah and her son Logan, while Syd's younger daughter Ginny circled the room snapping photos of the party. Syd and Mason had taken the remnants of despair and fashioned a family.

Alex sighed. Before Soeurs opened, they'd been four friends. Now they were six sisters. Alex couldn't wait to see what God had in store for the next eight years.